KENDALL RYAN

The Soul Mate

Copyright © 2017 Kendall Ryan

Copy Editing by Jennifer Echols and Tami Stark

Cover Design by Sara Eirew

All rights reserved. No part of this book may be reproduced or transmitted in any form without written permission of the author, except by a reviewer who may quote brief passages for review purposes only.

This book is a work of fiction. Names, characters, places, and incidents are either the product of the author's imagination or are used fictitiously.

About the Book

From *New York Times* Bestseller Kendall Ryan comes a sexy new stand-alone novel in her Roommates series.

The smoking-hot one-night stand I was never supposed to see again? Yeah, well, I might be pregnant, and he's my OB-GYN.

Prologue

Bren

I rolled over, allowing my arm to fall onto the mattress beside me.

Except there wasn't a mattress beside me.

No, when my arm fell, it landed on nothing but warm, solid muscle.

Crap.

I peered through half-closed eyes to see if the man sleeping beside me had noticed me move. If he had, he must have been doing the same thing as me, pretending to still be asleep, but based on the steady, rhythmic breathing, I had to guess not.

Carefully I sat up a little straighter in the bed, then glanced at my companion again. His full brown hair was mussed from sleep and the rest of his body was mercifully covered by a white down comforter.

Thank God for small blessings.

Because if I had one more look at those abs, those powerful thighs, and his other…impressive qualities, there was no way I'd be able to drag myself from his bed.

Which was exactly what I had to do. I just had to get up and get the hell out of here before what I'd done actually sank in. My car was still at the bar where we'd met, but I could take a cab…when and if I ever found my phone.

Shit.

I tried to mentally retrace my steps, thinking where it might have gone, but as I thought about the night before, my face flooded with heat and pleasure and just the tiniest hint of regret.

Not for what I'd done. I'd needed the chance to get out and unwind far too desperately for that. And no one deserved a pass from the judgment police more than me.

No, I regretted the idea that a night as hot and steamy as last night had been would never happen again. At least, not with this guy—whose last name I hadn't managed to catch.

My bad.

We'd walked into the apartment, electricity crackling between us like some kind of freakish magnetic pull. I'd barely gotten a look at the high ceilings and the chrome fixtures before he'd walked up behind me and…

I shivered and tried to get a grip.

Okay, if I started thinking about what he'd done, I'd give up the good fight, sink beneath these sheets, and give him the friendliest wake-up he'd ever had.

Which, again, I could totally *not* do with Mr. One Night of Fun.

With an internal chuckle at his new nickname, I shifted my weight ever so slightly, I started again, trying to push him from my mind and replaying only the images that were most pertinent to my getting home this morning ASAP.

My bra was on the floor beside me. My panties—I winced—were destroyed.

A little ache ran through me as I recalled exactly how they'd wound up that way, but I forced myself to focus again.

Okay. So, no panties. But my dress…my dress was crumpled on the floor in front of the front door. I remembered that much. So I just needed to hunt down my phone and purse.

I slid a little way from the stranger's heated skin, ignoring the pang of longing for a second—okay, fourth—time. Slipping on my bra, I tiptoed from the room, careful to open the door as quietly as possible and thanking everything that was holy for his silent, modern floors and doors that didn't make a creak.

When I opened the bedroom door and I saw one of the things that had impressed me about his place the most—the wall of solid glass overlooking the city—I realized I was standing in front of it with my hoo-ha hanging out for God and everyone to see.

Heart thumping in my throat, I snagged my dress from where it lay on the floor and shoved it over my head, letting out a little yowl when the hook caught my hair and tugged. I held my breath as I heard a little thud from the neighboring bedroom. *Please, you sexy beast, you, go back to sleep,* I willed him mentally.

My heart pounded against my chest as my ears strained, listening for the slightest sign of life. When it stayed quiet, I figured I was in the clear and went on the hunt for my shoes.

Okay, so we walked in the door, I had admired the apartment, I went to get some water and…and I slipped off my shoes. On tiptoe now, I sprinted to the sink and found my strappy sandals, then slid them on. Beside the sink, I spied a little notepad and pen hanging from the fridge and I chewed the inside of my cheek, willing myself not to reach for the pen to leave my name and number.

He probably would never use it.

And even if he did?

I thought again of that spark between us, the rush of animal need I'd felt from the first moment I'd spotted him looking at me from across the bar. He had a look in his eye that made me—probably made every girl—feel like I was the most important, luckiest woman to have been selected by him.

And when he spoke?

His deep, mellow voice felt like chocolate sliding over me, sweet and satisfying.

A guy like him? He wasn't looking for repeat visitors. In fact, he was nothing but a quick ride to Hurtsville, party of one.

Which was perfect. Because after everything I'd seen of guys? I wasn't on the lookout for more than a one-nighter anyway. But a girl still had needs. And if I could get them met while at the same time reminding myself about guys and their limitations? That was a win-win and if Mr. One Night of Fun were awake right now, he'd agree.

I backed away from the fridge and bumped into the island, only to find my purse directly behind me.

"Gotcha," I hissed as I lifted it, then fished through the tiny bag's contents until I found my phone and ordered a car.

Five minutes until it got here.

I glanced at the bedroom door again, wondering if it was rude not to say good-bye. After everything we'd done together last night? Lord only knew the kindest thing would be to let him sleep. Surely by the time noon came, I'd have forgotten all about him anyway.

Besides, it wasn't like I'd ever see him again. Nope. It was the kind of night that should be savored and then placed firmly in the past.

Chapter One

Mason

"What the actual fuck, Mason?"

I groaned as Trent's voice echoed through my foyer, then lay back on the couch and tried to pretend like if I didn't look at him, he wouldn't be able to see me. Which, of course, was bullshit. But I was fresh out of ideas.

"What day is it, motherfucker?" Trent's voice was louder now, closer, and despite my better judgment I cracked an eyelid open to find him standing over me, his normally dark expression even darker than usual.

"Leave me alone," I croaked.

"Nope." He shoved my feet off the end of the sofa to take a seat on the buttery white leather. "It's Sunday. And you want to know what happened? I was just fucking humiliated out there."

"Shit. Sorry about that." I turned, pulling my feet up onto the ottoman, then yanked my blanket a little closer to my chin.

"You are not," Trent muttered. "You know Sunday is rugby in the park. How the hell are we supposed to win a game without our star player? Today was Medical versus Surgical, you piece of shit. You think the surgeons are going to let us live this down? Ever?"

I winced, knowing he was right. Fucking surgeons, cocky pricks. Fact was, they shouldn't even have been playing rugby considering how precious they were about their delicate hands, but that didn't seem to stop them.

"Look," I said, feeling slightly bad for the first time since he'd basically broken into my place, "I'm kind of going through something right now. It's an emergency and—"

"Not being able to find the contact info for your one-night stand does not constitute an emergency, no matter how many times you try to frame it that way, Mason."

"One man's burden is another man's gift. Tomato, tomahto. No crying over spilled milk." I ran out of bad, inapplicable sayings and straightened up on the couch. Trent snagged the remote from my hand and muted the episode of *Treehouse Masters* I'd been watching.

"Still no luck, huh?" Trent asked, a little less harshly this time—though still not by much.

"Nope," I muttered, pinching the bridge of my nose. "I checked every dating site I could think of. She wasn't on any of them. I even looked on Tinder. Nothing. In fact, no one with the name Bren at all."

"Hey, here's an idea." His lips twisted into something resembling an encouraging smile. "Just go on a date with someone from Tinder and forget about it. It's been a week, dude. Let it go." Trent crossed his arms over his chest, and I reached for the bowl of lukewarm soup in front of me.

"You don't get it, do you?"

"That you discovered the holy grail of pussy? The pussy to rule them all? The fucking one pussy that obliterates all the rest of the pussy?" Trent snorted. "I *get* it, I just don't buy it." He shoved a hand through his thick, dark hair. "There are plenty of girls out there. I could even set you up with one of Kayla's sisters if you would just—"

"No, I'm *going* to find this girl." I clenched my fists, then blew out a ragged sigh. "It's just going to take a little more work than I expected."

I already knew I was spinning my wheels in vain trying to explain *her* to a guy like Trent. For him, every woman he dated was the same—a chance to get laid and, if he was lucky, have a good time before, during, and for a little while after. Maybe.

For me? It wasn't so easy.

Don't get me wrong. I could have just about any woman I wanted. That wasn't a cocky thing, either. It was just…well, the truth. Ever since I'd been old enough to know how sex worked, I'd been able to find willing partners, but for me relationships were about more than just a quick roll in the hay. Becoming a doctor hadn't hurt the situation, and loving women on the whole didn't hurt me any either.

And still, I wanted something *more*. Now that I was getting older…

Well, that *something more* seemed to be getting more and more important all the time. This girl had blown my fucking mind in the best possible way. She'd been gorgeous, of course. But she'd been funny, and smart, and unexpected. I'd gone to sleep totally satisfied and stoked to tell her exactly that in the morning, only to find she'd ghosted.

Gone, without a word or a note, even.

Trent slapped his knees and pushed himself from the couch before making his way to my fridge and pulling out a bottle of water. He twisted the cap off, took a slug, then eyed me over the bottle. "Okay, fine. I give. What's so special about this one, besides the steel trap of a pussy, that is?"

I cocked my head. "That's the thing. I can't put my finger on it. I mean, the sex was…"

There were no words for the sex.

From the moment I'd first kissed her, I'd been completely absorbed, lit with the need for more—to touch her, smell her, and breathe her in. It was more than chemistry—it was sheer animal connection, and I knew, even from that first, innocent kiss, that she could feel it too. Our connection was unlike anything I'd ever felt.

"It couldn't have been that good if she snuck out of here while you were still asleep. You'd think she'd want round two, right?" Trent shrugged. "Face it, maybe she's just not that into you."

"See, this is what you're not getting. She *was* into me. She was perfect." I shook my head.

Of course, I didn't blame Trent for not understanding. Odds were that he'd never been with a woman who looked at him the way Bren had looked at me on our date—like every word I said mattered to her. Like *I* mattered to her. In a way, it reminded me of the way my mother spoke to and looked at my father—like nothing in the world was more important than that other person.

And that connection had been only the starting point. It stretched even further when I'd kissed her, like the push and pull between our bodies was one we'd done a million times before but was still exciting and new. She'd shivered when I touched her, and when I turned her around to unzip her dress…

"Exactly. She was perfect. That's why she wasn't interested in you." Trent grinned and I chucked a pillow at his stupid face.

"But seriously, dude," he pressed on. "What are you going to do, just wait for her to knock on your door? You've already looked everywhere. It's time to give it a rest and try again. There are plenty of fish in the sea. And seriously, I've never seen you like this and you're starting to freak me out."

He rejoined me on the couch and I glanced at the TV for a second, thinking over his words.

It was true. When it came to women, I had…well…*a history* would probably be the most polite way to put it. But that wasn't technically my fault either.

I was raised with one belief, taught to me by my parents and reinforced by their actions toward each other—when you found the right person, you knew. With that one right person, all the trials and tribulations of life became easier.

And me? I wasn't going to stop until I'd found Mrs. Right.

So, I'd experimented. A lot.

"If you'd had sex like this with a woman like this, you would be acting the same way," I said, fully confident in my words.

"At this point I'm starting to think her vagina was made of solid gold," Trent said. "What did she do? Blow bubbles out the damn thing?"

I laughed. "It was good, man. Best sex of my life. Hot and intense, and that fucking mouth—"

"Right. Well, special as it sounds, it's time to move on. Got it?" Trent took another sip of his water and I nodded, though it was purely in the interest of placating him.

In truth, I didn't think there was a damn thing in the world that could make me stop looking for the mysterious Bren.

Even now, a week after the fact, my mind's favorite place to wander was the memory of her perfect, cherry-tipped tits and her smooth, pale skin. Her silky blond hair between my fingers. Her responsive, writhing body.

And, of course, the taste of her pussy as I'd laved my tongue over her straining clit.

At this point, even her name was enough to get me hard as a rock. But it wasn't enough—none of it was.

Because I *was* going to find Bren.

And when I did?

I was sure as shit going to make her mine.

Chapter Two

Bren

I'd done it. I felt like high-fiving myself.

Whistling the tune of "Baby Got Back" as I washed flecks of poo down the drain, nothing could dampen my mood.

I'd had a one-night stand—a damn good one, in fact—and like a mature, responsible woman, I'd kept the no-strings promise I'd made to myself. *Booyah*. Smiling again, I felt proud of myself. And satisfied in a way I hadn't been in a long time.

It was only normal that my mind had wandered to Mason a few times throughout each day over the past two weeks. It was the only sexual experience I'd had in what felt like a decade, and so it was natural that I'd want to replay it—my own personal highlight reel, something to remember fondly and enjoy when I was in bed, alone at night.

"Why are you in such a good mood?" Mandy asked, peeking into the gorilla's night house.

Hosing down one last oversized log, I turned and shut off the water. "Hey, lady. How was vacation?"

Mandy was five-foot-nothing of pure sass and sarcasm. I loved her. She was technically my boss, but it never felt that way. I was grateful for her friendship and all the guidance she'd given me both at work and in my personal life.

Mandy smirked and me and shook her head. "I'll tell you all about our *trip* in a minute. When you bring two toddlers on a plane, it's not a vacation—it's a trip. But first, you're going to tell me why you seem positively enthralled to be cleaning up shit. Isn't Andy here today?"

"Yeah, I told him to go have his lunch. I've got this."

Her eyes widened. "The hell you say? Let's go catch up inside. You can fill me in on what happened while I was gone."

After coiling the hose and putting it away, I followed Mandy inside. The gorillas weren't due back inside their enclosure until this afternoon, but I was happy to be done with that task early.

I shucked off my rain boots, leaning for a moment to steady myself on the wall. *Whoa.* A wave of nausea washed over me, and I sucked a deep, cleansing breath into my lungs. That was the third time today that had happened.

Shaking my head, I followed Mandy toward the workstations, and after washing my hands at the sink, I sat down on the stool next to her.

"Now, spill it, Bren," she said, grinning at me like she knew something I did.

"Fine." I shrugged. "I took your advice. Are you happy?"

She pumped her fist in the air. "You got laid! I'm so proud. Give me all the squishy details. And leave nothing out. Todd barely has the energy for sex anymore, and when he does, I have to be in the mood to deal with his beer belly."

I inwardly shuddered. The idea of holy matrimony had never interested me, and Mandy sure as shit wasn't selling it. Honestly, I didn't want to fall in love. It just didn't appeal to me. I saw all the negatives and none of the positives. Being single with a great career as a zoologist was more than enough for me. It didn't take years of therapy for me to figure that my dad passing away when I was young and my mom falling into a deep depression had shaped that view. But, hey, I got lonely sometimes and a girl had needs. Hence my magical one-nighter.

"I was thinking about what you said—about

needing to put myself out there more. I considered online dating."

Mandy grinned. "But?"

"Filling out that long profile and answering hundreds of random questions was so daunting, and I didn't like the idea of putting all my personal info on the Internet. It just didn't seem necessary to exchange names with someone I merely wanted to exchange bodily fluids with."

Mandy patted her heart. "Sometimes you make the feminist inside me very proud."

I rolled my eyes. "So I figured before I went that route, I wanted to try things the old-fashioned way first. I got dressed up cute and went to a bar I never normally go to—you know, one of those young, hip, way too crowded places?"

She nodded, totally absorbed in the story. "A meat market is the technical term, yes."

"I sat alone at the bar, sipped my drink, and made eye contact with a couple of cute guys around the room. A few minutes later one of them came up to talk to me."

Her eyebrows wiggled. "And bow-chicka-wow-wow?"

I laughed. "Not exactly. He was cute, but he

didn't get my blood pumping. After I made an excuse about needing to go to the restroom, I spotted the most gorgeous man I'd ever laid eyes on sitting alone in a booth in the corner. He looked so unhappy, and I thought that was so odd—like the two of us were the only ones in the entire club who were just enduring this scene rather than partying it up like everyone around us seemed to be."

"Hmm." She nodded thoughtfully. "Then what happened?"

I closed my eyes for a moment, and it was almost as if I was right back inside that club, the bass of the music pulsing through my veins, the handsome stranger's electric blue eyes locking on mine from across the crowded room—the hair on the back of my neck standing up when I realized he was even more attractive than I'd first realized—and then ducking my chin to scurry away—sure that no man in his class would ever been interested in me.

"A few minutes later, when I came out of the restroom, I was ready to call it a failed mission and head home. But Mr. Tall, Dark, and Sexy was waiting for me."

As a delicious shiver traveled up my spine, I recalled the way he'd towered over me, even in my wedges, and the commanding edge to his voice when he asked if I'd like to get a drink with him. I'd merely nodded, my voice trapped beneath the weight of my libido.

"He led me to his private booth in the back, where we ordered another drink and talked."

Mandy frowned. "If this story doesn't end with you taking it up the honeypot, I'm out."

I laughed at the unusual euphemism. "I'll speed things up for you." Mandy didn't need to know about the way the conversation had flowed so easily that night, or the current of raw sexual tension snapping between us with every barb we exchanged.

"A little while later he asked if I'd be interested in going someplace quieter, where we could talk. He suggested his place, and off we went. His apartment was gorgeous—one of those glittery sky-rise places that towers above the city."

"I'm jealous—did this hunk have a name?"

"Mason." Just the feel of his name on my tongue provoked a response in my body I wasn't ready for.

"Then what happened? Don't spoil the fantasy and tell me his meat-stick didn't measure up. There's nothing worse than a tiny wiener, am I right?"

"It was an absolutely amazing night. Perfect in

every way."

"Sweet baby Jesus… You've got to give me more than that!"

I shook my head. "I am not telling my boss every gritty detail of the best sex of my life." Only because if I remembered it with that much clarity right now, I'd soak my panties while at work. No bueno.

"Damn, girl. I've got to give it to you." Mandy reached her fist out to bump mine. "I'm all proud and shit." She faked a choked-up voice and had me laughing again. "Now I see why you've been in such a good mood."

It was crazy what good sex and a couple of orgasms could do for the soul. It was two weeks later, and I was still positively glowing.

Mandy and I worked in silence for a few minutes, her happily clicking away on the keyboard as she replied to a couple of emails, and me completing the log to note the time I'd done the interior pen cleanup earlier.

That nauseous pit was back, lurking in the center of my belly.

"That's weird," I muttered to myself.

"What?"

I shook my head. "I'm sure it's nothing, but…" I

paused, my eyes fixating on the calendar in front of me as a cold panic crept down my spine. "No, it's nothing. Couldn't be."

"What's nothing?" Mandy pressed again.

"I just, I've been having these waves of nausea for the past couple of days."

"Are you sick?"

"No. I feel fine during the day—for the most part. It's usually just first thing in the morning when I get out of bed and then a couple of random times throughout the day. It's probably a low blood sugar thing."

Mandy looked skeptical. "Bren. I don't mean to scare you, but those were my exact symptoms during my first pregnancy. You and this mystery man used protection, right?"

"Of course. We used a condom."

"But your cycle's late, isn't it?"

I guess my wide-eyed glance at the little desk calendar had been sort of obvious. I nodded. "By a couple of days. No big deal." But it felt like a huge fucking deal. I could not be pregnant—not by some one-night stand suave player who picked random girls up at the bar. *No, no, no. That only happens in bad rom coms.* My hands went clammy and I started to sweat. As the world spun around me, I considered the implications of having my perfect life imploded by an unplanned pregnancy.

Mandy licked her lips. "Listen. I don't mean to freak you out, but maybe you should go in to the doctor—get checked out. Condoms break all the time. It's possible you could be pregnant."

"I'm sure it's nothing. I can pick up one of those over-the-counter tests on my way home tonight if it makes you feel any better."

Mandy shook her head. "Those tests aren't reliable so early in pregnancy. Let me call my guy. Seriously, I have the best gynecologist in the entire city. I freaking love the guy. He normally has a six-month wait list for taking new clients, but a friend got me in, and maybe I can do the same for you."

"What's so great about the guy?" Call me crazy, but I had a hard time believing one could actually have an enjoyable experience at the gyno's office. I barely tolerated my annual visits. That cold metallic feeling of the speculum, and that awful K-Y Jelly. *Ugh.* No thank you.

Mandy's gaze softened and she got this faraway look in her eye. "He's smart, sweet, and professional, and he just has this way about him that makes you feel comfortable. Everyone loves him. And his office feels more like a spa than a clinic. Low lightning, soft music, plush cotton robes instead of those horrible paper napkins they used to make me wear at my old doctor's office. They have a freaking cappuccino bar in the waiting room. You'll love it, I promise."

"It does sound nice." I chewed on my thumbnail. "And it would be nice to know, I guess, what's causing this nausea."

Mandy nodded and grabbed her cell phone from her back pocket. "Let me see if I can get you in next week. No promises."

I waited anxiously while she dialed and spoke to the receptionist. She spelled my name and then waited on hold for a few seconds. Mandy's eyes widened as she checked the clock. "Yup! She sure can. Thank you so much!"

"What'd they say?"

"They had a cancelation this afternoon. You're in! You have an appointment with Dr. Bentley at two."

"Wow. Okay, and you're all right with me leaving early, then?"

She waved a dismissive hand at me. "Of course I am. Call me the second you know something."

The nauseous feeling was back, but this time it

didn't have a thing to do with the possibility of being pregnant.

Chapter Three

Mason

"Nine pregnancies," I told Trent as I leaned against the counter.

"Nine?"

"Yep, nine. And two sets of twins. I'm telling you, if I get one more pregnancy this month, I'll win the nurse's baby bingo league. Mrs. Ramirez cried for half an hour when I told her about the twins. She already has a pair at home."

"That poor woman." Trent gave a sympathetic wince and shook his head. "I'm going to grab a coffee. You want one?"

The lure of caffeine called to me, but I shook my head. "Nah, I'm so behind on my paperwork. Gonna catch up before lunch."

We parted ways, and I trailed down the fluorescent-lit hall until I reached the office at the end. "Dr. Bentley" was emblazoned on the door in shiny gold.

The name placard had been there since I was a kid, when I'd played in the waiting room and waited for my father to come out and join my mother and me. Then, when I was older, I'd spent even more time in that same waiting room, insisting that I go along for every little screening and test while my mother battled through ovarian cancer with one of the other doctors in my father's practice.

And now? As an adult, I'd taken control of the office that had once belonged to my father and replaced his certificates and diplomas with my own—though I'd left the old baseball pennant that hung from the window, a memory of my good old little league days.

On my desk sat the pile of papers I'd been avoiding for a solid week, and as I collapsed into my worn leather chair, I let out a muffled groan. Almost on instinct, I checked my work email and pushed aside the little stab of disappointment when nothing even remotely personal was there.

Not that I'd expected anything at this point anyway. If I hadn't heard from Bren by now, I wasn't likely to. In fact, I wasn't even sure she knew my name. I'd introduced myself once at the beginning, but some people were bad with names. I often was, forgetting them almost the second a stranger told me. Plus I had no way of knowing how tipsy she was that night. Of course, she hadn't seemed drunk at the time.

My cock pulsed at the memory.

Scrubbing my hands down my face, I tried to forget what it'd been like with her. Not that it did any good. I hadn't slept a full night since we'd been together when she hadn't found a way to infiltrate my dreams.

Speaking of dreams, if you want to be able to pay for that fancy-ass apartment and a bed to lay your head in at night, you better get on the ball with this paperwork.

After a quick email to my assistant, asking her to order my lunch in, I flipped over to the first sheet in the stack of papers—Mrs. Ramirez's intake form from this morning.

Poor woman was right. I could only imagine what it would be like to have one baby, let alone to be saddled with two more when you already had a pair at home. Her husband had stayed strong, of course, but if I'd been that guy? Well, I think we would have made an extended stop at the liquor store after a doctor's visit like that.

She was a great mom. I'd seen her during her aftercare when she'd had the first set of twins, and she'd been like a superwoman, on top of their every move, rocking one while patting the other. The parents would be all right once they adjusted, but damn, that was going to be a motherfucker of an adjustment. Hoped they didn't like sleeping at night.

A gentle knock sounded on my door, and I looked up to find a slender brunette woman slipping into the room, a nervous smile on her thin lips. "Dr. Bentley?"

"What's up, Jean?" She was the newest of the nurses and still referred to all of us by our titles even when we weren't in front of patients, so I tried to make my smile extra friendly.

"There was a cancellation this morning, and we had someone fill the spot with a new patient. I know you've got a lot on your plate, but I was wondering if maybe—"

I held up my hand. "No problem. When's the appointment?"

"Um, that's sort of the thing. She's here now."

I made sure not to wince visibly, knowing Jean was already walking on eggshells due to nerves. I didn't want to make it worse. "Right, okay. Well, draw her blood, take her vitals, and get her into a gown. I'll be in as soon as I can."

Jean started to leave the room, but I called her back.

"The intake form?" I asked, and she let out a shrill laugh as her cheeks flamed red.

"Right, right. Duh! Here you go." She dropped the slip of paper on my desk along with a medical history folder, and I glanced at the tidy, pretty script.

Ashley Matthews.

Pretty normal history and on the younger side. I flicked through the pages in her folder, then sent off the last few emails in my inbox before heading back down the hall. Trent was going to owe me for taking on yet another new patient. If he was smart, he would bring back a coffee for me regardless of the fact that I didn't go with him.

Gently, I knocked on the door, and Jean appeared from around the corner.

"Dr. Bentley is here," she informed the woman who was lying like she'd recently been hit by a truck. Her hair was slung over the side of the examination table, and her arm was flung dramatically over her face.

This ought to be fun.

Chapter Four

Bren

"Not feeling well?"

A deep male voice interrupted my nausea. My churning stomach was as insistent as a gnat buzzing near my ear, and I just wanted to slap it away. But in order for that to happen, I had to subject myself to this exam. Damn the comfy robe that Mandy thought I'd enjoy. If I had the usual paper sheet covering me, I could just pull it up over my head.

"Ugh," I groaned, and the nurse piped in.

"Miss Matthews isn't the biggest fan of…lady doctor visits."

"Can we…uh… just get the uncomfortable part over with as soon as possible, please?" I added in a strangled whisper, still not removing my arm from over my face. Another flip of my churning gut caused a moan.

"No problem. I totally understand."

Why did the voice sound familiar?

The doctor ran the water in the sink, and I peeked out from underneath my arm mask in time to see his rigid back. The snap of the rubber gloves sounded like gunfire to my sensitized body. I closed my eyes once again. God, could this just be over with already? There was nothing worse than the annual stirrups of shame, and now I had to be subjected to it *twice* in one year. And if I was pregnant? I'd have so many hands inside my hoo-ha, I could tattoo an *open for business* sign right above it.

"Please scoot down to the end of the table."

That voice.

If I hadn't been so miserable, I would have garnered the energy to peek at whoever was looming over me. Instead, it took everything inside my soul to move down until my bare ass was hanging over the end of the table. A hand gripped one foot, then the next, helping me place them in the dreaded stirrups, but I kept my knees pressed firmly together.

The light creaked, and then it snapped on. Its searing heat pierced my sensitive flesh, and I felt on display. Exposed.

Vulnerable.

"Okay, Miss Matthews, I'm just going to—"

"I've had an exam before. I know the drill," I groaned. If I could have flashed a green light in his face, I would have. Anything to speed up this torture.

"All righty then, let's not waste any more time." With gentle hands, he pushed my legs apart. "Relax, this will all be over soon."

The doctor pressed on my stomach and slid two fingers inside my vaginal canal. Just when I thought he'd hurry up and get it over with, he stopped. My heart raced, and my already sweaty palms moistened to the point where I thought they might drip onto the paper lining the leather exam table.

Why was he stopping?

Was something wrong?

With me or with my possible baby?

He exhaled a ragged breath that spoke volumes. Something was definitely off here. I opened my mouth to speak, but nothing came out. White-hot panic seemed to have frozen my tongue.

A prickle of realization laced with dread stole up my spine and landed on the top of my skull.

"Bren?" he murmured softly.

My rapid breathing slowed to a stop as the tension in the room ratcheted up to Defcon Five.

"Yeah?" How did he know to call me by my middle name? Something about his voice sounded vaguely familiar. I racked my brain and slowly pulled the arm from over my face. If I could just get a good look at his expression, I might be able to gauge how devastating this situation had become in the space of a couple of seconds.

"Is everything o—"

My gaze met his, and the room spun. A wild, tragic swirl of vibrant colors took the place of regular vision. I struggled to sit up but fell back down on my back with a whooshing thump and a crinkle of paper.

No. Fucking. Way.

This can't be happening. It can't. God, what did I ever do to deserve this? The humiliation? The mortification. The...

"The form said your name was Ashley," he said as a dose of adrenaline hit my system, causing my pulse to hammer wildly.

Shit. It was *him*.

And his fingers were still inside me.

Another wave of nausea flowed over me, and I shut my eyes against the light of the fluorescent overheads, begging my stomach to stay calm. If I could just control my breathing, I could get the hell out of here without totally losing it.

"Can you please remove your hand?" I managed.

"Right. Sorry." The doctor slid his thick fingers from my lady parts and rose to his feet.

After at least a minute of ragged inhales and prayers directed at my stomach to not shame me any further, I managed to moan out, "My name *is* Ashley." I scuttled back on the table and covered my legs. He may have seen it all before, but in the cold light of the exam room, I felt more exposed than I'd ever been. "I go by my middle name."

Snapping off his gloves, he tossed them into the trash can. "Right. Uh, Jean?" He turned to face the confused nurse who looked like she'd entered an alternate universe and didn't understand her role there. "Would you mind giving us a moment? I'd like to speak to Miss Matthews alone."

"Sure, I'll just…" Jean cleared her throat and opened the door, but as she backed out of the room, I didn't hear the distinct click of the metal door closing behind her.

Pinching his nose between his fingers, he dragged himself from the edge of the exam table and snapped the door shut himself before turning to look at me again. I didn't think I could withstand the implications of that look.

Shit. What did it mean?

I'd already taken my feet from the stirrups and sat perched on the end of the exam table, the white paper crinkling beneath me as I shifted restlessly. I stared at a spot on the pristine tile floor, focusing my attention there.

God, I wished that he'd just get out of this room so I could put my clothes back on and erect some type of fabric barrier between us. He had the upper hand, and he knew it.

"Listen, I should probably go. I had no idea—" I started, but he cut in.

"Why did you just disappear on me like that?"

I should have known he wouldn't be a gentleman and let me escape with at least a shred of my tattered pride intact. My cheeks flushed with color under the blame lacing his words, and I could feel it creep from my neck upward. I swallowed hard but kept my lips clamped together. How dare he ask that question right now?

"I had a great time with you," he admitted after a strained moment. "I…" He blew out a breath and raked all ten fingers through his hair.

Nothing mattered more to me right now than getting out of this exam room. It felt like all the oxygen had been vacuumed out. I couldn't draw a normal breath.

"I—"

"Did you not feel the same way? Because I thought—"

"No, no." I shook my head, and my long hair fell over my face before I pushed it behind one ear. Considering leaving it hanging over my eyes like a veil, my hand trembled under the effort of the simple motion of securing it back so I could see him. "I had an amazing time too. I just…" I shook my head, trying to find words that made sense. "You were—are—more than I'm looking for. Right now, I mean."

"What does that mean?"

"I'm just…" I took a deep breath, not finding the appropriate words to explain how I felt about our night together. How did one explain to a medical doctor while naked on the exam table that they weren't looking for a father for the unborn baby they might be carrying? Especially, when that father was *him*. "You're…that night…everything was so intense, and I'm just not interested in anything serious."

"Based on one night, you decided it would have to be something serious?"

Why couldn't he be like every other man led around by his dick and just get over it already? I felt embroiled in some kind of strange role reversal. We didn't need to be having this awkward conversation. He could have just remained professional, finished my exam and never seen me again. No harm, no foul. I didn't care that he'd given me the best sex of my life. I didn't. I really didn't. Now, here he was doing his version of damage control, trying to keep me under his thumb and seeking a compromise I didn't need or want.

I tilted my head to the side. "I was just looking to unwind and have some fun. It's not something I do often, but to be honest, I'm surprised you even wanted to see me again."

"So, which is it? I'm too serious, or I'm such a player you thought it wouldn't matter if you just disappeared?"

"Why can't it be both?" I countered.

He clenched his jaw and narrowed his eyes into slits, clearly unwilling to accept my pretzel logic. "Because it doesn't make any sense."

"I had to blow off some steam and so did you. We both had fun. We don't need to make it into something more, do we?" I shrugged but glancing down, I could see the tremble in my hands that gave me away. Hear the lie in my own voice.

He stared at me, as if seeing me for the first time. Was I the same woman that had been so soft and pliant in his arms weeks before? No. The reason I was here, naked and vulnerable and exposed to his gaze made me night and day different from that woman. I might be pregnant. My future might depend on some positive sign in some sterile lab. I had to make him think that I felt as if he were nothing. Nothing more than a whim—a quick, easy fuck, something that could be tossed aside in the morning and forgotten.

But in my heart, I knew the truth. I'd felt it. That hot, coursing electricity at every move and touch. My heart practically exploded when we'd come, hard and needy and deep, together. That look in his eyes while he was inside me…that hadn't been in my head. It couldn't have been.

It *wasn't*.

"Okay, so, if it was just a one-night stand—" he started, but I cut in before he could finish. I couldn't let him say something we'd both regret.

"It was."

At my careless words, disappointment lined his chiseled features. I almost felt bad for deliberately hurting him. But not enough to make it right by spilling the truth. Doing that would leave me open to heartache. And mine had bricks around it that even a battering ram couldn't break through.

He took a steadying breath, and after a few measured moments, a mask of cool indifference came over his face. "Right. Okay. It was just a one-night stand. So we should probably just continue with the annual exam. It'll be super quick, and then a nurse will call you in a few days with your Pap results, all right?"

"Uh." I swallowed hard and then speared him with a glare. Was he dense? Now, I had a whole other can of worms to open up.

"Look, I know you're probably a little uncomfortable, but I can be a professional. You are here for the annual exam, correct?" He glanced down at the chart again. Maybe I wouldn't have to spell it out. If he forced the issue, I didn't know if I could tell him the reason for my visit without breaking down. As he scanned the document, everything appeared fine until he got to the bottom. If I hadn't been about to throw up and pass out, I might have enjoyed the tragic look on his face.

Now who feels like puking, huh?

He paled. All the color and blood drained from his face, and he wobbled, his six foot plus frame swaying like a willow in the breeze. Slowly, he dropped back into his rolling stool, then steadied himself against the counter.

He looked at my face, searching. Trying to determine if I was joking. As if. Women my age didn't joke about something so serious. I narrowed my eyes and held his gaze.

Do you get it now, Einstein? If there's a baby, you're the father. Which means if I'm really pregnant and want to keep the baby, in nine months' time, you're going to be someone's dad...

After breathing in deeply through his nose, he opened his mouth to speak, but before he could delay the inevitable one second longer, I hopped from the table and grabbed my panties from the chair beside the table.

"Look, uh, this was a bad idea." I shoved one leg into my jeans, having slid on my panties in record time. "I can find another doctor, I promise. Mandy was only trying to help me out. I didn't know this was your practice, obviously, and I just...I need some air."

I hopped into my jeans and buttoned them, then reached for my top.

He opened his mouth to say something but remained silent after a couple of strained seconds. I half expected him to start yelling at me about condoms and birth control pills. As a doctor, he had to be wondering how this happened. But he should know, because condoms could and did fail. Obviously.

"Don't worry about it, really," I said before he could get going with the platitudes and false promises. That was the last thing I needed. "It's probably a false alarm, but if not, you know, I know where to find you, so…" I let out a humorless laugh as I turned around and ripped off my robe before shoving my shirt over my head. Now that I stood before him, completely covered, I almost felt better. But nothing short of getting the hell out of this tiny, suffocating room would help me draw a normal breath again. "Please, just pretend I was never here."

His mouth came unhinged again. I seemed to keep striking him speechless, and I prayed he'd remain that way while I emulated a magician and disappeared. I slipped through the door, nearly sprinting for the lobby with sure, purposeful steps.

Before I reached safety, that deep voice halted me in my tracks.

"Bren, wait. We need to talk about this."

My feet seemed to have become cemented to the floor. Why couldn't I just be rude and leave? Shove him firmly in my past again like I did before? Something about the man caused me to act so out of character, I barely recognized myself. He awakened too many feelings in me that I wanted to stay dead and buried.

"I'll deal with the consequences myself," I said in a low voice, not turning. If I looked at him, I'd stay. So I tamped down the desire to fling myself into his strong arms and stepped from the room and into the wide linoleum atrium outside the door. I could almost feel his breath grazing the back of my neck.

Why won't you just give up?

Before I could reach the sidewalk, he reached out and turned me around, forcing me to look at him.

"Running isn't an option anymore. Whatever this is, the lab already has your specimen sample from when the nurse took your blood. The results are coming, and when they get here, I won't let you face them alone. No fucking way."

Chapter Five

Mason

I could tell by the tight line of Bren's mouth that my expression had turned into a scowl. Her hands trembled, and emotion practically poured from her eyes.

Of all the doctors in the city, how in the hell had she ended up in my exam room for a pregnancy test? Damn. It was right what they said about Karma being a bitch and all that.

I racked my brain, reliving every single second we spent together, realizing I never told her my actual profession. Not wanting to sound like an arrogant douche, I rarely led with that in a bar or club. Besides, being a doctor with my own practice made me a moving target for gold diggers and clingers, so I was absolutely positive I hadn't told her who I was.

My fingers itched to reach out and gather her into my arms so I could wipe that heartbreaking look off her face. But I didn't move because I was still a little pissed that she'd ghosted me after the best night of my life.

Her eyes gazed into mine, seeking something. Something I couldn't yet give. Promises I couldn't make. After staring for several strained seconds, she took a step backward.

"Can we please go talk in my office?" I asked, my voice slightly more controlled.

Becoming agonizingly aware that we were still standing in the lobby, I took a deep breath and tried to compose myself. An older woman stared slack-jawed at us, and a young mother rocked a newborn in a baby carrier, trying hard to ignore the spectacle in front of her.

My gaze passed over the decaf cappuccino bar that Trent had promised would soothe our patients, making them more comfortable once they got to the exam table. Suddenly, I wished my life was as simple as deciding between the salted caramel or mocha syrup. I let out a long breath, calmed my temper, and turned back to face Bren. A woman running from me caused a pit to form in my gut because it felt like the worst kind of rejection, especially when I'd done nothing to deserve it.

"I'm sorry. I can't. I have to get back to work." Before the last syllable left her mouth, I knew she was lying to me. Any woman as upset as Bren looked in this moment was headed for a phone call with her bestie and a pint of Chunky Monkey. All I wanted was the gym and a drink. Only the sting of serious liquor would help sweep the memory of what just happened from my mind.

Pregnant.

With my baby.

The implications weren't lost on me. Bren could have life growing within her womb as we stood here not talking. Even though our interactions had been brief and physical, I could sense her independence. She probably didn't want to be saddled down with responsibility and tied to a man who just a while ago had been a perfect stranger.

Bren's face turned white as a sheet, and she sucked in a huge breath. "I feel like I'm going to be sick."

I grabbed her elbow and pulled her toward the door emblazoned with gold lettering that read LADIES as she rushed for the toilet bowl.

She heaved once, twice, but the contents of her stomach stayed put. As Bren turned her head toward me, I knelt down in the tiny stall beside her, my hands sweeping her hair into a makeshift ponytail.

When she stood, I took a step back. "You all right?"

She nodded and swiped at her mouth with the back of her hand. "False alarm, I guess."

"Have you been getting sick?" I asked, suddenly more worried than I had been.

She lifted a shoulder. "Just a little nausea."

"You sure you should be going back to work?"

Come back to my place. Let me take care of you.

As she stepped out of the stall and washed her hands, I didn't speak the words that popped into my mind before any others. Once I got back to my office, I'd sink into my buttery leather chair and consider how much I wanted this woman and our unborn child playing a starring role in my future.

"I may just head home. The day's almost over anyway," Bren said, backing away from me almost as if she thought I'd corner her in the ladies room.

"And you'll be okay to drive?"

"Yes. I don't live far from here."

"Okay." I rubbed one large hand across her shoulder, and she took another uneasy step back. The physical rejection stung worse than a hornet's bite. I really didn't want her driving home in this condition, but I couldn't think of a rational way to get her to stay or let me put her in an Uber.

Of their own accord, my facial muscles tugged downward, but I dropped my hands to my sides in defeat.

I almost felt like grabbing a few paper towels and waving them in the air above us like a white flag. "I'll call you later. We need to talk about this."

"All right. My cell number is on the form I filled out."

My hands clenched into fists at my sides as I felt completely frustrated and incompetent. If I couldn't protect the mother of my unborn baby, what good was I? But I picked myself up by my bootstraps and followed her to the door.

"Talk to you later, then," she said and pushed open the door, her feet carrying her like a crazed stalker was on her tail. I watched Bren's rigid and retreating back until her body became just a speck of nothingness off in the distance. My heart throbbed like someone had cracked my chest open without the benefit of anesthesia.

After Bren's blood draw earlier, the lab would take twenty-four hours to get the test results back. I'd be on pins and needles until the results were in. Which meant I had a full twenty-four hours to ruminate about Bren.

Leaden feet led me back to my office where I shut the door and inhaled. Focusing on paperwork helped, so I shuffled through a pile and waited a few hours to call her so she could have time to process and calm down.

The Soul Mate

I knew I'd be useless until things were settled or at least discussed between Bren and me, so I suggested dinner. How emotional could she get in a public place? Once I got her on the line, I could tell by her hesitation she didn't want to see me. Too damn bad. So I pushed.

"Sure," she mumbled, giving in.

Glancing at the clock on my desk, I blew out a frustrated breath. I still had an hour before we were supposed to meet. Plenty of time to go to my apartment to shower and change. This was going to be the longest twenty-four hours of my entire life until those test results came in.

In the meantime, I needed a plan. I needed to push everything else out of my mind so I could focus on Bren and getting to know her. Make her want to know me.

I tented my hands and touched my fingers to my lips.

You can run, Bren Matthews, but you can't hide.

Chapter Six

Bren

I didn't go back to work. Couldn't, because then I'd have to tell Mandy what happened, and I figured if I didn't say anything—out loud, to anyone—I could pretend for a little while longer that this whole sordid afternoon was a grainy figment of my sleep-deprived imagination.

I didn't want to have a random stranger's baby growing in my belly, didn't want to be saddled down with responsibility and tied to a man I didn't even *know*. What if he didn't like romantic walks on the beach and candlelit dinners? What if he was a typical workaholic and every night he came home dead tired, after hitting the gym and then collapsed onto the couch with the remote control in his hand?

What if he tried to rein in my freedom?

When the phone rang a couple of hours later, I about jumped out of my skin. Even though he'd said he'd call, I'd been consumed with my jumbled emotions so hadn't really been expecting it, or his invitation to join him for dinner. I tried like hell to think of an excuse. But I wasn't good at lying on the spot, and so I'd mumbled a weak "Sure."

Glancing at the clock above my kitchen sink, I blew out a frustrated breath. I still had an hour before we were supposed to meet at the restaurant. This was going to be the longest twenty-four hours of my entire life. I wanted to hit my knees and pray for a negative result. If I wasn't pregnant, I could get rid of him and his unwelcome effect on my equilibrium. Trying to push the pending results out of my mind, I stood in front of my walk-in closet, gazing at the endless options I had hanging inside. Wearing stained khakis and my assigned polos to work every day meant I liked to splurge on girly things like handbags and sandals and dresses from time to time.

But now I was surveying my closet for an entirely different reason—since I only had a one bedroom apartment, this is where the baby would sleep. I'd have to have it remodeled to accommodate a crib and changing table and all the other unknown essentials a tiny human required.

Finally deciding on a skirt and cardigan combo, I headed toward the front door, steeling my nerves for what was sure to be an awkward *date*.

I couldn't shake from my mind the memory of the slashes of Mason's dark eyebrows pulled into a scowl this afternoon. I'd never expected to see him again, especially not with such an irate expression on his face. But his angry expression wasn't what had shaken me to my core.

No.

It was unexpected, but that wasn't what had me so shaken.

I couldn't believe that of all the doctors in the city—Mandy had sent me straight into the stirrup-laden clutches of the one man I'd been trying so hard to forget. And during all the time we'd spent together, Mason had never mentioned what he did for a living. Even worse than the shock and awe was his massive effect on my already shaky body. Every line of his handsome face, every plane of his chiseled body, slayed me right through to my soul.

Those sapphire blue eyes framed in dark lashes had blazed on mine, and I'd been at my most vulnerable, unable to steady myself, wanting more distance between us. As if widening the physical gap would sever the magnetic pull I'd felt from the moment our eyes had locked across a crowded club. Even after I'd dressed and fled to the lobby, he'd given chase. A sturdy, square jaw dusted with stubble, and powerful shoulders that jutted out wide, then tapered down to a trim waist. The man was perfection, and that was without allowing myself to remember what was beneath those baby-blue scrubs. Placing my hand on my belly, I said a silent prayer that I could make it through this evening without succumbing to his charm.

I'd been through too much and couldn't go down that road again. He may have missed the neon sign on my heart practically flashing *CLOSED*, and it would be my job to remind him. I wasn't looking for anything. We'd had one night of fun, and now look where I was. I'd just have to put on my big-girl panties and deal. Like I always did. Ridiculously hot doctor be damned.

Chapter Seven

Mason

I didn't feel right not picking her up and driving her to the restaurant like a gentleman. Hell, Bren could be the *mother* of my unborn child. But then, of course, nothing about this whole situation felt right—not my clothes, not the way it happened, and certainly not the way it might end up. But then, well, maybe it really was fate.

I glanced at my phone, knowing it wouldn't tell me anything my internal clock hadn't told me already.

Bren was late. Which left me to sit here, wondering if I'd been stood up.

When I'd called her earlier today, she'd sounded willing enough—no doubt she wanted to plan out what would happen if the results came back the way she expected them to…the way we both expected them to.

But then, on some level, I thought we both already knew the answers. I would be there with her, take care of our baby, and make sure her delivery went as smoothly as it could. I would help her and I would love our child. There was no question I would be there for my baby in every way I could.

What was less certain was how she and I would do. How we would get along aside from our one night of hot, passionate sex. Even though my gut told me it was right, I had to admit I didn't really know her at all. I knew her body well enough. But I needed to get to know the woman attached to it.

Before this baby came—if it came at all—I wanted to get to know *her*. Wanted to see if the reality lived up to the fantasy I'd built up in my mind about who Bren could be to me.

The one.

My phone buzzed on the table in front of me and I glanced at it. When I saw it was from Bren and read the word *"here"*, I breathed a sigh of relief. Glancing around, I spotted her standing in the bright sun pouring through the glass doors. I waved her over to the table I'd requested near the wide bay windows overlooking the water.

She offered me a nervous smile, then headed over, hitching her purse on the back of the chair before settling into the seat opposite me. "Fancy place," she said.

I nodded. "Hope you don't mind. They have the best Arnold Palmers here, and since you're probably not drinking, I thought…"

She bit her bottom lip, a soft pink glow taking over her cheeks. "Thanks. That was thoughtful."

A long silence stretched between us, and I glanced out at the water just as a fish jumped into the air and splashed back down.

I know how you feel, buddy. Less than five minutes and I'm already floundering…

My mind raced, searching for the right words to say to fill the awkward pause. Something that wouldn't give her any reason to want to run away from me. Bren dug through her big bag and pulled out a stack of crisp white papers. "Look, uh, I know this is weird, but I drew up some ideas for custody and—"

I took the sheets and set them aside. "I get that and why you want to do it, and if it turns out that's necessary, I promise I'll look at them. But it's jumping the gun, to say the least. I don't want to talk about the elephant in the room," I said. "We had a good first date—let's consider this the second. I just want to have a nice dinner and get to know you."

Bren's wide eyes conveyed her surprise. Maybe she thought we'd get right down to business. *Surprise. Bet you didn't consider that I wouldn't allow you to build another wall between us.*

"We didn't do much talking that night once we left the bar," Bren murmured, though her shoulders seemed to relax a bit as she settled more deeply into her chair. "But sounds like a good plan anyway."

A waitress came by and took our drink orders, and as Bren perused the menu, I grabbed a roll from the basket between us and began to apply a liberal amount of butter. "So, you know I'm a doctor."

She let out a little yelp of laughter. "That became pretty obvious when you walked into the exam room when I had my legs in the air."

I grinned, stunned at how warm that little laugh made me feel inside. "Yeah…that was regrettable." She'd discovered I was a doctor when I had my fingers inside her. "But anyway, what do you do for work?"

She glanced at me over the menu. "You don't want to get me started on it."

"Why? Are you a secret agent? If you tell me, you'll have to kill me and all that."

She chuckled, and I caught a flash of her pretty white teeth. That smile. Dammit, it might be the death of me because I felt heat tingle from my scalp to my toes as I stared at her mouth. "No, my friends just always regret asking me about my job because I never shut up about it, so I'm warning you now. Back away while you still can."

"I'll consider myself warned. Now, what do you do?" I asked again, even more interested now that I knew how passionate she was about her work.

"I'm a conservationist at the zoo here in the city." She beamed, finally loosening up and giving me a glimpse of the real Bren. The one I wanted to get to know better. "It's the best job in the entire world."

Her enthusiasm was infectious, and I found myself grinning back at her again like a fool. Jesus, this woman did something crazy to my insides, and I sure as fuck didn't hate it.

"That's sounds like a really awesome job. Tell me more."

She nodded, her hair falling over her face as she popped a chunk of bread in her mouth and chewed before continuing. "Mostly I work in the cheetah enclosure. They're fascinating animals. You know, we pair them with dogs because on their own they actually get really lonely, so it's this precious thing where the dog thinks he's the alpha and he eats before the cheetah and almost leads his buddy, and the cheetah and the dog become like besties. It's amazing."

"Are you serious?"

She nodded again, her eyes bright. I swallowed as I imagined her naked beneath me, looking up at me with that same hypnotic gaze. "Each pair sort of has their own personality."

"So, which is your favorite?"

"Cocoa and Nibs. Nibs is a chocolate Lab and Cocoa is his cheetah best friend. They were born on the same day and they do everything together. You've never seen anything more adorable in your life." She pulled her phone from her purse and slid it closer to me before pressing the central control and showing me a picture of two animals spooning while they slept—a chocolate Lab the big spoon and a cheetah the little spoon.

"That would break the Internet if you posted it. And blow people's minds. Cats and dogs are not supposed to act like that," I said, genuinely impressed. "That's amazing. How did you not tell me all this before?"

"Like I said, I get a little caught up and I don't want to monopolize every conversation, so I have to watch myself. But I'm done now, really. Tell me more about you."

The waitress reappeared with our drinks and I took a sip while considering her. I wanted to know more about her days—how she spent them, which of the animals she liked the most, but I also didn't want to pressure her.

"Um, let's see. There's not a whole lot to know. I'm a doctor. I've lived in the city my whole life. My parents live here too."

"Yeah?" She tilted her head to the side. "That must be different, never having moved away from your parents. I wonder sometimes if that's the way to do it. My mother is always saying how much she misses me."

"Well, honestly, I didn't have much of a choice. I was going to go to Johns Hopkins when I graduated from high school, but my mom actually got really sick, and I felt like I needed to stick around for her through that."

Her full lips folded into a frown. "I'm so sorry. That's awful. Do you mind me asking what happened?"

I nodded. "Ovarian cancer. They were sure she would…well, you know." I knocked on the wooden table, a rush of emotion making my gut clench in a vice-grip like it always did when I thought of how close we came to losing her. "She's fine now, though. My father nursed her through and made sure she went to all the best doctors and received top-notch care. You've never seen a doctor work so hard for someone who wasn't his actual patient."

"Your father is a doctor, too?"

"Yeah," I took a sip of my drink, worried that I sounded like the kind of dipshit that couldn't think for himself. I'd always just knew I'd follow in my dad's footsteps. But work like Bren's? That was pure passion which echoed through her every word and gesture. "It was a family practice, actually. I did my internship at the office, and residency in the local hospital and then, when my dad was ready to retire, I took it over, just like he did with his dad."

"Wow. That's an incredible legacy." She smiled, but suddenly a note of tension re-entered the space between us. Like she *knew*.

I cleared my throat. "That was more happenstance than anything. We all just happened to find fulfillment in treating patients."

"I can understand that," she said, nodding. "I see the vets come in and care for the babies or the sick animals and it feels very" —she paused for a moment before adding—"noble."

"Thank you." A little rush of heat surged through me at the smile that lit her face, and I glanced away, trying to shove the memory of her writhing beneath me from my mind.

This wasn't about that. This was about getting to know each other the way we should have that first night.

I couldn't seem to knock the devil off my shoulder who insisted that just because we started the night differently tonight didn't mean it couldn't end the same way. Me between those silky thighs, that tight pussy clenching over me as she called out my name.

I coughed and shifted in my chair to ease the sudden pressure behind my zipper and shot her a smile.

"We'd better figure out what to order."

Before I shit-canned this whole dinner idea and ordered another helping of Bren Matthews.

Chapter Eight

Bren

I'd never wanted a glass of wine so badly in my entire life.

Though, of course, I would have taken a shot, too. Or maybe a hole in the head. Anything to get me off this constant roller coaster or to make me less likely to hide under the table until he finally gave up and left.

Swallowing hard, I forced myself to remember what he'd just asked me but was saved when the waitress stopped by our table to take our order. "Uh, the apple, bacon, and gorgonzola salad, I think. Sounds good. Not that I'm like craving apples or anything."

He nodded. "It does sound good. Steak for me, please."

He ignored my complete spazziness just like he had earlier. Which, of course, made perfect sense.

Because that's exactly what he was—perfect.

Seriously, not only had this guy completely rocked my world in bed, but now he was telling me about his close family ties and how he stayed in the city to take care of his ailing mother? What was he going to say next, that he was up for sainthood after performing his next miracle?

"What's on your mind?" His deep, rumbling voice broke through my thoughts and I looked up at him, feeling weirdly like those clear blue eyes of his could see through me and into my mind.

"What?"

"You have a weird expression on your face. I was just wondering why. What's going on in your head?"

"Oh, uh" —I cleared my throat—"it's silly."

"Something about the animals?"

"No." *Damn.* Why hadn't I just said yes? That would have been the perfect out.

"Then what?" He laughed.

I glanced around and finally huffed out a sigh. "This is going to sound stupid."

"I doubt it."

"Well, then, if you have to know, I was wondering why you're still single."

He raised his eyebrows and I rushed to finish my thought.

"I mean, you're handsome and successful. You're a doctor. You must have women falling all over themselves to get to you, and you see hundreds of women in your office."

"Dating a patient is not an option," he said. "It's unprofessional, not to mention unethical."

"Okay, fine," I murmured, slicing my hand through the air. "Other than that, though. You have to have had women fawning all over you, and you've got these stories about bringing babies into the world and taking care of your sick mom and all that, so, like, what's the deal?"

"What's the deal?" he repeated, and his eyebrows hitched slightly higher. Taunting me. Why couldn't I make sense while talking to him? I'd had just about enough of stuttering Bren and wondered when poised Bren would come out of hiding.

"Yeah. Why aren't you already taken? You're what…thirty?"

He cleared his throat again. "Thirty-two."

It seemed ludicrous. Unless, of course, he was already taken and hadn't felt it pertinent to fill me in on that fact. I toyed with my fork trying to act nonchalant as I waited for him to respond.

He rubbed at his perfectly chiseled jaw. "Well, I do date quite a lot."

"That still doesn't explain why you're single."

He eyed me and then took a sip of his drink. "Look, I'll tell you the truth, but then I'm going to be the one sounding silly."

"Seems only fair at this point, considering the level of awkward I had to suffer through on your exam table," I fired back.

"You got me there." He tipped his head in a clipped nod. "The reason I haven't settled down with one person is because I'm looking for more than just sex and companionship." His intense gaze burned into mine as he leaned forward, and I barely suppressed a shudder. "It's going to sound cheesy, but the fact is, I want a soul mate. Someone who not only loves me, but understands me on my deepest level, you know? Accepts me for who I am, faults and all. After watching my parents all my life—and especially through my mother's illness—I just think life is too short to waste it on anything less."

A lump knotted in my throat.

Life *was* too short.

I thought of my own parents—my father's illness and after. But then, maybe Mason's rose-colored glasses only existed because he hadn't seen the other side of that struggle…the devastation when the struggle was finally over and there were no winners.

I wasn't sure if my parents had been soul mates, but they'd been in love. And now my mother was alone and heartbroken, so downtrodden that she could barely function without my father around to help her.

So, yeah, life was too short. Too short to fall head over heels for someone and then wind up totally destroyed when that person disappeared from your life in one way or another.

But I wasn't about to get into all of that. Especially not with him—not now. He already knew more of me, both inside and out, than I'd meant to share with him. It was time to pump the brakes a little and get back on more solid ground. If I could just gain a little more control over an untenable situation, I'd start to feel better.

He talked about his favorite parts of his job, and we laughed over TV shows we'd both seen and books we'd read, but in the back of my mind, I was still replaying what he'd said.

He wanted a soul mate. Someone who knew his deepest self. I'm sorry, but that scared the ever-loving fuck out of me.

I couldn't deny that I'd felt something the night we'd been together—sure. But that had all been animalistic, greedy need. Sheer, unadulterated attraction. Hell, that was half the reason I'd run out of his place like my butt was on fire.

What were the odds that some random one-night stand he'd potentially managed to knock up would be his soul mate? The one person he'd been waiting for?

Not freaking likely. Plus, add to that the fact that I might be sticking him with a baby, and then what? A guy like this would stay by my side, try to make it work, and settle even if I wasn't his soul mate. Settling wasn't an option. Not for him and sure as hell not for me.

He was a catch and a romantic all rolled up into one, and there was no way it could work out. At least, not with someone that had walled off her heart years ago. I couldn't give him what he wanted. And I wasn't even sure I wanted to if I could.

The whole idea of what might happen had my stomach tied in knots and before I knew it, we were wrapping the rest of my salad to go and heading through the restaurant's wide glass doors and into the sunset-lit parking lot. He followed me to my car, the orange and pink of the sky bouncing off the white sedan, and when I reached the driver's side, he stopped to face me.

"So, what's the verdict, Bren? Are you feeling okay?"

I knew he wasn't referring to the queasiness I'd mentioned, which came and went. He was talking about our real first date—he was asking how I felt about *us*. The truth was, I really didn't know. He was handsome, intelligent, kind—and amazing in bed. But I didn't really know him, and this baby would speed things up to an unnatural pace, and that terrified me.

"It was a nice dinner. Thank you for that."

"Right. Well, I'm going to go out on a limb and take that as an invitation to call you again."

He leaned down and my body froze. I knew I ought to back away—not get sucked in by his sweetened spicy smell, but his eyes were locked with mine and I found myself moving closer, letting my mouth close over his soft bottom lip.

His tongue didn't sweep out to greet me. Instead the kiss was soft and sweet, but the feel of his skin on mine sent a wave of white-hot energy through me, along with a surge of memories of everything that mouth of his could do—everything he'd already done. Everything I wanted it to do again. And again.

But even as I started to melt into him, he pulled away.

"Good night," he said, his voice all grit as he backed away and opened my car door for me, waiting as I climbed inside.

I watched him climb into his own car in a daze, my mind reeling.

Jesus, he was like a drug. One taste and I wanted to mainline him straight to the vein.

I had to get a grip. Clutching the leather steering wheel, I closed my eyes. The kiss had been a mistake. This whole date had been a mistake. Jesus, why did the best night of my life have to turn into my biggest regret?

But I would be okay. I was walking away knowing one thing I hadn't been sure of before—this guy, whatever his romantic intentions toward me, would be a great father. That was more than I could have hoped for after a one-night stand. This baby—if there really was one—would be lucky to have him. That was what I needed to focus on. This wasn't just about me anymore.

I drove on autopilot, playing the date in my mind over and over until at last I arrived home and put myself to bed. Tomorrow would be a new day and I made a mental vow it would be free from any lingering thoughts about Mason Bentley.

We wanted different things in life. Until I found out if I was pregnant, it only made sense to continue to talk. But I'd spend the time between now and the next time I heard from him shoring up my emotional and physical defenses.

Something told me I was going to need them.

Badly.

Chapter Nine

Mason

"How is it I always find myself standing in front of you, asking the same question?" Trent walked into my office unannounced, almost catching his lab coat as he snapped the door shut behind him.

I set down my sandwich on my desk and glanced at him. "And which question is that?"

"What the actual fuck, man?" Trent raised the clipboard in his hand then dropped it down in front of me.

"What?"

I glanced at the chart.

"Mrs. Ramirez. You filed her paperwork all wrong. In fact, everything you've touched this morning has been fucked in one way or another and the nurses are blaming your assistant and your assistant is blaming the nurses. Before all hell breaks loose with every employee of the female persuasion, tell me what's going on?"

I scrubbed a hand over my face. "Shit. Okay. I'll look at the files and fix everything. I'm sorry. I'm just a little distracted today, that's all."

"No kidding. You've asked Jean seven times if the hematologist reports are back. Do you think someone has leukemia or something?"

"No, not that." I blew out a sigh, then pushed my sandwich away from me before motioning to the chair in front of my desk.

"You remember the girl I was looking for? Bren? The one who—"

"Snuck out of your apartment like you'd been holding her hostage? Yeah, I remember. You about to tell me you tracked her down and don't know what to say?"

"Oh, I talked to her. Yesterday when she came in to see if she was pregnant."

Trent's jaw slackened. "You're shitting me?"

"Oh, how I wish that were the case, because it was awkward as fuck, but nope. It definitely happened."

"And you're just telling me this now?" Trent demanded, spearing me with that betrayed and pissed off look like I'd just violated the man-code.

"There's nothing to tell for sure, yet. I didn't want to be an alarmist," I reasoned, kicking back and stretching my legs out in front of me.

"When you couldn't find her after your night together, you deemed it a dire emergency, holing up in your apartment like a pussy-whipped fool. Now she might be pregnant and you decided it wasn't worth mentioning?" His voice had hopped up an octave as he stared at me, incredulous.

"When you say it out loud it sounds stupid," I admitted with a half-smile.

"So, you're waiting to see…" Trent started.

I nodded, finishing his sentence for him. "…to see, when her blood results come back to find out if she's pregnant."

"So, what are you going to do?" Trent leaned back in the chair and folded his hands in his lap. "You seem pretty chill about the whole thing, weirdly enough."

"Only one thing to do. If she's pregnant, I take care of the baby and figure out how to be a good dad."

"Obviously. But what about her?" Trent pressed.

I leaned my head back, staring at the tiled ceiling for a long moment before answering. "That's the thing, isn't it? I like her—"

"I remember that much."

"But I mean, I really like her. We went on a sort of impromptu date last night, and I like who she is as a person. I want to get to know her more, but with this baby thing between us and not being sure how she actually feels about me, it makes things way more complicated."

"Well, seems like it would make her want to make it work, right?" Trent shrugged.

"Exactly why I want to get to know her better before we find out about the pregnancy. There's no way to know our real feelings. Once those test results come in, we'll never know if a natural relationship could have developed between us. We'd always wonder if we were just trying to make things work for the baby."

"I don't get what's so wrong with that," Trent said. "We've seen plenty of couples who are trying to make it work because they got pregnant."

"I know that. It's just that don't want either one of us to settle, you know? If we didn't know the results—if there was some way of keeping the possibility of a baby out of the equation—we could date like normal people and see if there was a chance. If not, no hard feelings. And if so…"

"Then you know it's the real thing with or without a baby." Trent nodded. "Sounds good to me. So just don't look at the results, then. Seems simple enough."

"Are you kidding?" I said with a harsh laugh.

"No. What do you have to lose? She wants to keep the baby regardless, right? So what's the harm in waiting a little longer?"

I thought back to the stack of custody papers she'd handed me on Friday night. "Yeah, she does."

"What difference does it make, then? She gives up drinking for a month. You put the results in an envelope and date until it's time to open the thing."

"But if the pregnancy is ectopic or something—"

"Then I'll know the results and run things smoothly as they normally would go," Trent said. "Now, I came in here to tell you the hematologist just dropped off this week's tests. What do you want me to do?"

My stomach clenched into a tight knot. Could I live with not knowing about the baby for an entire month? If it meant I got a shot at developing a real relationship, naturally, with Bren, then the choice was easy. For me, at least. I just hoped she'd let me lead in this situation.

"I guess pitching her the idea couldn't hurt."

"It can't. I'll go take care of everything." He pushed himself from his seat and strolled from the office, and I stared down at my half-eaten sandwich, suddenly no longer hungry.

Could I really do this? As badly as I wanted to rip into that envelope, I knew that Bren deserved to be the first person to know.

More for something to do than anything else, I picked up the sandwich on my desk and took a bite, barely tasting the food before swallowing it. In a matter of minutes, Trent returned, a sealed, unmarked envelope in his hand.

He sat it on my desk on top of the clipboard holding my litany of mistakes. I wondered if he'd done that on purpose.

"Here you go," he said, his tone totally flat.

I searched his face, but he looked impassive as ever.

"What?" I asked.

Trent shook his head. "I told them not to tell me unless there was a pregnancy *and* a potential problem. Only one person in this office knows the truth and I'm not telling you who it is."

"Right." I nodded. "Smart," I muttered, impressed in spite of myself.

"Now, you should probably call your girl. I imagine you've got some talking to do."

Trent slipped from the room again, and I glanced at my phone before pulling out Bren's intake form and dialing the number there. The phone barely had a chance to ring before her clear, crisp voice sounded on the other end.

"Hello?" she said, her voice washing over me like honey.

"Hey," I started, "it's Mason."

"Oh, hey." The nervous spark in her voice heightened. "Do you have the test results?"

"I do, and everything is fine, but I think we should talk about it in person. Is there any chance you could meet me in my office this afternoon when you get out of work?"

"It's my day off," she said. "Is there a time you had in mind?"

I glanced at the clock. It was nearly one—not time to go home. But then, Trent did owe me a favor or two…

"I'll have my partner cover my appointments for this afternoon. Could you come in now?"

"Um, sure. You said you're sure everything is okay?"

"I'm sure. I just think it'd be better to talk in person."

She agreed and hung up, and then I forced myself to take a deep breath and focus on the work in front of me. With a quick note to my assistant, I asked her to work my schedule around. Then I stared at the intake and patient records I'd ruined earlier that day.

With any luck, not knowing for the next month might get easier. But right now?

Right now I kept staring at the clock every few minutes, waiting for the buzzer to sound and let me know that Bren had finally arrived. After ten torturous minutes, though, it finally did.

"Let her in," I told my assistant, then sat up straighter in my chair as I waited for the door to creak open and Bren's pretty, heart-shaped face to peek around the corner. When it did, I had to bite my tongue to keep from breaking into a huge grin at the sight of her.

It felt like all the oxygen had been sucked from the room. In washed-out shorts and a faded blue blouse, she was knockout. Her hair was long and wavy today, and her wide-set gray eyes stood in stark contrast to her pale skin.

Due to nerves or morning sickness? I couldn't help but wonder.

"Please, sit," I motioned to the chair Trent had occupied before and she settled in easily, though she hitched her purse a little higher on her shoulder rather than setting it on the ground. I double-checked to make sure the door was closed, then picked up the envelope containing our combined fate and handed it to her.

"What's this?" she asked, then moved to open it, but I stopped her.

"Wait," I said, holding up a hand. "I have a proposal, and you can decide whether you want to open it when I'm done, all right?"

Chapter Ten

Bren

Two minutes after he was done with his little speech, I was still blinking back at him in stunned silence.

"So, let me just get this straight," I said, finally finding my voice. "You want to wait until I'm almost two months pregnant to find out if I'm pregnant at all?"

It sounded ridiculous—ludicrous, even. I had to be missing something.

But no, he just sat there with those clear blue eyes staring at me, as if this was the most obvious solution on the planet.

"I've thought a lot about it and I think this is the only way." He nodded. "To know if there's definitely something here that has nothing to do with this potential baby, which I think there is."

"Right." I took a deep breath and stared down at the envelope. "I guess…I just don't see why it matters. Like, either we get along and everything is great or we don't and then have seven months instead of eight to figure out how we're going to raise a baby."

Both of which, of course, were terrible options.

After all, I didn't want to see where this led. Hadn't I told him as much by sneaking out that night? And hadn't I made that loud and clear when he'd asked me about it at dinner?

He was a nice guy, a romantic. A hot, successful doctor with a heart of gold and magic hands.

He was exactly the kind of guy a girl could fall for.

If a girl wanted to fall. Which I, most definitely, did not.

"I just don't think either of us should settle," he said. "If we find out that we have a baby coming, we'll want to make it work between us for the baby's sake."

"Or we could never try and successfully co-parent because we never crossed that boundary to begin with," I countered, half hoping he would agree and half hoping that he'd shut me down.

He tapped his fingers on his desk, staring long and hard at the wood before his gaze rose to mine again.

"Do you really think that's an option? We're going to spend years co-parenting together not knowing what it's like to be with each other again—after everything that happened that night—and we'll both never have a moment of weakness and want to find out? Maybe you can, but I know I sure as fuck can't."

His gaze burned through me, and again I remembered the heat of his body against my skin, the weight of his as he moved on top of me, filling me with so much pleasure I felt like I could explode.

I swallowed hard, tamping down any lingering desire. Dismissing it as irrelevant to our future. "The attraction is not something I can deny," I admitted.

"So this is the only way. The right way. Let's see where it goes."

"But if we have a baby on the way, there are things we need to discuss. Giving up a whole month just to pretend this isn't happening—"

"Then let's not. If it's that important to you to get a plan together, let's go somewhere and set one up. You and me. Once all that is laid out, we'll be able to continue not knowing. Unless, of course, you hadn't planned on keeping the baby?"

Automatically my hand moved to my stomach, and I considered what he'd said. The words had been free of hurt or judgment, and I knew he was allowing this to be my decision, but the choice had already been made. In truth, it had never been a question at all for me.

"I'm keeping it," I said. "If there's a baby."

He nodded. "If there's a baby."

He held out his hand and nodded toward the envelope, and I handed it to him. He stuffed it in his pocket, shrugged off his lab coat, then moved past me to the row of hooks behind my chair. Picking up the leather jacket hanging there, he put it on, then held out his hand to me again. "Now let's go. Time's a-wasting."

I followed him, and together we walked through the office, through the atrium of the building, and finally out onto the street, where a friendly row of shops greeted us.

"You like frozen yogurt?" he asked.

I nodded.

"Good. There's a really good place over here." He nodded toward a little shop with a pink awning. We approached it, and then he held the door open for me.

I stepped in and stared at the wall of options, momentarily overwhelmed.

"They have dividers," he said. "You can get more than one."

He handed me a cup with four-way divider in it and I went to town pouring pistachio, coconut, chocolate-covered pretzel, and salted caramel yogurt into my cup. When I was done, I met him at the buffet of toppings and noticed him shoveling chocolate-covered raspberry jellies onto a massive serving of chocolate yogurt.

"Chocolate lover, huh?" I asked.

He nodded, then made for the brownie bits like he'd never seen anything so decadent before in his life. "For sure."

"I'm more of a yogurt purist." I squirted fluffy whipped cream on top of each of the sections of my yogurt, then set it on the scale for the friendly-looking cashier.

"I've got it," Mason said, "Just give me a minute."

He stopped in front of the hot fudge canister and poured a healthy dollop on top of what had to be a two-thousand-calorie dessert.

If I'd been worried about having to be super healthy around him just because he was a doctor, his actions blew that theory out of the water. We were going to be ourselves, and that made me smile.

When I looked up, I saw the cashier eyeing him like she wanted to devour him, and a surge of jealousy coursed through me before I got hold of myself again.

"All set," he said, then shelled out the money to pay for our treats before making his way to one of the little white tables in the front of the store.

I grabbed a cheery-looking magenta spoon and joined him at the table, ready to dig in.

"Okay, so, down to business." He took a spoonful of what had to be pure hot fudge, then said, "You want to talk about the baby. Let's work it all out so you won't need to worry about it for at least a month."

"Well, there's the complex stuff." I played with my pistachio yogurt. "Like, I'll need to learn a lot. I'm an only child—I don't have much experience with babies. I'll need to consider looking into classes and such."

"I've got you covered." He shrugged. "I know everything about babies. When your milk comes in, the benefits and detriments of nursing, all of it. I know every stage of pregnancy backward and forward."

"Right." I tilted my mouth to the side. "But what if something is wrong?"

"I have a friend who will look after you just to be on the safe side."

I took a deep breath. Okay, that made sense. "And what about the other stuff…the exciting stuff?"

"Like what?"

I shrugged. "I don't know. Picking out a name. Picking out colors for the nursery. I won't get to do any of that. Plus, what if you really want to name your son after yourself and I want a different name?"

"Something wrong with the name Mason?" He raised his eyebrows.

"No, I just had a different name in mind."

"What's that?"

"For a boy, it's really important to me to name him Jacob." It had been my father's name, the name my parents would have given me if I'd been a boy. The name my brother might have had if my father had lived long enough to have another child.

"What's so special about Jacob?" he asked.

It was the perfect chance to tell him—to explain why I couldn't be his one and only, even if I'd wanted to. But I wasn't ready for all that just yet. I couldn't open my heart like that—especially not to someone who was still relatively a stranger.

"It's a family name," I said simply.

He nodded. "Jacob it is, then. Problem solved."

I chewed on my bottom lip. "I picked the boy name. Feels only fair you pick the name for a girl."

"That's easy. Gwen."

"Gwen?" I asked. I didn't mind the sound of it. In fact, it was even kind of cute.

He nodded again. "It's my mother's name. I think she'd be honored."

"Settled then. Gwen or Jacob." I stabbed my spoon into my yogurt, trying to ignore the completely overwhelming feeling that—now that this baby had a name—everything was all too real. Which, of course, it might not be.

But then…

If it was, didn't I owe it to my child to give his or her father a chance? It might destroy me in the process, but then…didn't all parents make huge, life-changing sacrifices for their children?

"Okay," I said. "We'll do it your way. But you keep the envelope. If I have it, I'm going to rip into it. I can't live with the temptation."

He gave me a solemn nod, but the envelope was only half the temptation. Now that I'd made my decision, it was sort of open season, at least for now, on the good Dr. Bentley.

And the thought excited me almost as much as it terrified me.

Chapter Eleven

Bren

His warm tongue laved against my straining nipple, causing another moan to rip from my throat.

"Enough teasing," I groaned.

A warm male chuckle vibrated—against my inner thigh this time. "So bossy," he murmured. "I want to take my time with you."

His hot tongue met the oversensitive spot between my thighs, and any further arguments died on my lips.

Gah!

Digging my fingers into his hair, I tugged slightly, loving the way it felt to be in this position at all.

One-night stands weren't supposed to be like this, right? It was like someone designed this man just for me. He took his time hunting out every secret spot that made me shiver and then lingered there until I was desperate and trembling with need.

"One more," he whispered, the stubble from his jaw brushing between my thighs in the most distracting and delicious way. "Come once more for me and I'll give you what you want."

"Then let's get the show on the road." I lifted my hips, raising my warm, wet center straight to his mouth.

He chuckled again before diving in with gusto. His tongue could have set Olympic records with how skilled it was, and how embarrassingly fast he brought me to the edge.

"Mason!" I cried out his name, already there—right at that blissful moment before the most intense pleasure crashed through me—for the third time since I'd found myself in his bed.

He rose to his knees, his long fingers replacing his mouth, stroking in slow circles. He continued to hold me there—just at the edge—as he quickly covered himself with a condom.

"I want to feel you come this time," he said on a groan as he entered me. My body tightened around him, the invasion intense but oh so welcome.

His thick length speared me, and my entire body tightened. Deeper still he slid, and I cried out, so close.

"Right there," I said. "Just like that."

"You feel so perfect. Now come for me," he sighed.

I opened my eyes.

No, no, no!

I groaned in frustration.

I sat up in bed—alone—covered in a thin sheen of sweat, my heart pounding and panties soaked through.

The best sex of my life, and it was only a dream.

Holy shit. I just had the most realistic fantasy about Mason. I'd relived some of our steamier moments from our night together.

But my overheated body couldn't tell the difference between a sex dream and the real thing.

Turning over on my side, I punched my pillow into place, wondering how in the world I'd get back to sleep now.

***

"Can I ask you a question?" I glanced at Mandy over the surgical mask I wore, my voice muffled.

She was disinfecting a cut on the inside of a sloth's hind leg. Poor little guy.

"'Course. Anything. You know that." Her eyes behind her thick tortoiseshell frames narrowed on mine.

Drawing a deep breath, I steeled my nerves. "Tell me more about growing a human inside you."

Mandy set down the gauze she'd been using and grabbed a bottle of disinfectant. "You'll have to be a little more specific than that. What about it?"

"I had this dream last night. It was so vivid."

"Yeah, I remember having some crazy dreams." Mandy nodded. "What about?"

Glancing down at Mr. Pokey, I stroked his fur softly, a smile quirking up my lips. "Yeah, this was no ordinary dream…it was more of a vivid flashback of my time with Mason."

Mandy set down her tools, her eyes meeting mine. "Oh my God."

"What?" Her intense scrutiny gave me chills.

She took a deep breath, and we moved away from our patient, removing our rubber gloves and throwing them in the trash.

"I almost don't want to tell you this…but when I was pregnant, my libido was out of control. I was so horny. All the time. Poor Todd. I had a big belly, so sex was awkward, but that didn't stop me from begging him to take me from behind." She chuckled, clearly remembering something I did not want to know about.

At this new information, my mouth pulled into a frown. None of what she was telling me was making me feel any calmer about my situation. I figured my odds of being pregnant were fifty-fifty, but every time Mandy spoke, it was like I learned of another new symptom to freak out about.

With this new information, my chances of not jumping Mason's bones the next time I saw him were, what? Slim to none.

I was so screwed.

Chapter Twelve

Mason

"Almost done," I called as someone knocked on my door.

My assistant always got antsy at this time of day—not that I could blame her. By rights, she should have been able to leave an hour ago.

The door creaked open and I glanced up to find Trent standing in the doorway, a bottle of pills in his hand.

"What's up? Something wrong?" My heart rate ticked up a few notches, but Trent shook his head.

"Just some prenatal vitamins. Just in case." He shook the bottle, then set it on my desk. "You seeing her anytime soon?"

"I was going to stop by the zoo on my way home, actually, so I'll bring these with me."

"The zoo?" Trent raised his eyebrows.

"She's a conservationist there. Works with the endangered animals."

"You nerds all know how to pick each other."

"You're a nerd, too, dude" I pointed out.

"That doesn't mean I like my women brainy."

"I'm pretty sure your only qualification for a date is that she have a working vagina. And a heartbeat."

"Even that isn't a deal breaker. I'm happy to do a little extra work." Trent winked and I let out a little laugh.

"Right, well, I'm…so glad I know that now." I moved the paper I'd been working on into my out-box and shrugged off my lab coat in favor of my leather jacket. "Come on, walk out with me."

Together we walked down the carpeted hall to find that the rest of the nurses and assistants had already left for the day, and I shook my head as I locked up behind myself.

"Guess they all had places to be," I said.

"On Friday night? No kidding," Trent said.

"Who asked you?" I shot back. "Actually, I'm shocked you're not on your way to some hot date."

"Hell, no. Ever since your last hot date, I'm worried that I'll wind up like you."

"Handsome and successful?" I asked.

"Strapped to the train tracks of parenthood, my friend. No thank you. I can't wait until they come out with a pill for men. There aren't enough condoms in the world to make me feel safe after all this."

I rolled my eyes. "I might be having a baby. I'm not enlisted in a war."

"Oh, but you are. It's a field of land mines and pitfalls waiting to happen, my friend. I wish you the best of luck with your little situation, but I wouldn't trade lives with you for all the money in the world right now," he murmured, tipping an imaginary hat in my direction.

We reached the parking lot and said our goodbyes, and I made my way to the zoo, thinking over Trent's words. In truth, I'd never seen parenthood as an obstacle or a curse like so many of my male friends. To me, it seemed like a gift. Something to look forward to—so long as you were sharing the load with the right person.

Again I thought of the envelope sitting in the drawer of my bedside table. The night before, I'd held it in my hands, staring at it for at least an hour while I thought about the rest of my yogurt date with Bren. She was funny, smart, beautiful. Everything I'd want my child to be.

But she was still, in so many ways, a stranger.

And that needed to be fixed.

I pulled up to the zoo and snagged a space in the front row of parking before making my way through the gates. When I reached the ticket desk, I said, "I'm looking for Bren Matthews?"

The thin man behind the counter nodded but tapped the buttons on his keyboard all the same. "Twenty dollars, please."

I reached in my wallet and fished out a bill before slapping it on the counter and waiting for my wristband. The man handed it to me with a too-wide smile, and I nodded.

"Thanks."

"Enjoy your visit."

I walked through another set of gates and glanced at the directory, trying to remember what Bren had told me about her day. Though now that I thought about it, I remembered that she'd hardly told me anything at all.

No, she'd mentioned only the cheetahs—which meant I had only one place to look.

When I got to the exhibit, a man stood on the outside of the glass-enclosed cage, writing on a clipboard as he surveyed the animals. He was a tall, handsome kind of guy with slicked-back blond hair and a square jaw. Almost like the villain from any '80s movie ever made.

"Excuse me," I said. "Do you know where I can find Bren Matthews?"

The man looked at his watch, then nodded. "Carlisle went into the nursing enclosure about twenty minutes ago. If I were a betting man, I'd say she's there."

I frowned, not sure what Carlisle had to do with anything or who he was, but I nodded and gave him my thanks before following the signs that led to the nursing enclosure.

When I got there, I found a tunnel of leaves and a big, hand-painted sign announcing the newest babies at the zoo—Nancy the koala, Ferdinand the wombat, Henry the baby orangutan, and Daisy the baby gorilla.

I stepped inside the little space and spotted Bren immediately. Nestled in her arms was a baby animal. Bren fed her a bottle with the gentlest expression on her face, nodding as the man beside her spoke.

This guy, too, was blond and handsome, though less tall and tanned than the one I'd just met.

"The thing drives like a dream," he was saying. "You'll have to come out with me and try it some time. I'll even let you drive."

Bren nodded, lips curved into a smile. "Maybe sometime."

I raised my eyebrows and cleared my throat, fisting my hands at my sides because I felt like throat punching him. In my heart, Bren already belonged to me and this guy's blatant flirting irritated me to no end. "Hey."

She looked up and her cheeks flushed a pretty pink, although she didn't take the bottle from the tiny pink creature. "Oh, hey. What brings you here?"

I resisted the urge to hand her the clearly marked prenatal vitamins from my pocket to get her colleague to stop drooling over her but instead forced a grin. "Just thought I'd stop by to see you in action."

She cocked her head and nodded to the baby pig in her arms. "Well then, welcome to my world."

Her companion glanced from me to Bren and back again, his face falling a little. "You want me to take over?" he asked, gesturing to the pink.

Adorably dressed in a diaper, the pig was nestled in close to Bren's chest and she leaned to press a kiss to its nose. "It's okay, sweetie. I'm not going yet." She turned her attention to the man in front of her. "I'm good from here, actually, if you want to go punch out."

"Oh, uh, yeah. I was gonna get going anyway." He shoved his hands in his pockets and skirted from the little enclosure. "I'll see you on Monday, Bren."

"'Kay, see ya," she said to the other man, who hesitated and spent one moment too long staring at her.

Yeah, see ya, chump.

The guy, I could only assume was Carlisle, looked so deflated as he trudged away that, for a second, I almost felt sorry for him.

Almost.

I pulled the bottle from inside my jacket and handed it to her. "Actually, the other reason I came was that I thought you could use these. Just as a precaution."

"Oh, uh, thanks." She went a little pale as she balanced the formula bottle and pig in one hand and snatched the bottle of pills with the other. She shot a look around before quickly shoving it in one of the many pockets of her khaki cargo shorts.

"I didn't mean to interrupt," I said.

"No, no, we're just finishing up for the day. It's time to punch out, but I like to feed the babies before I go."

I shot a glance at Carlisle's retreating back in the distance and then faced Bren again. "How long has he been after you?"

"What?" she scoffed. "Carlisle? Are you serious?"

"He was asking you to go for a ride, and I'm pretty sure his car is option B. Option A was a ride on his d—"

"I get your meaning," she cut in, her cheeks turning red. "But Carlisle isn't like that. We're just friends."

She set the baby pig back in its pen, treating me to a glimpse of her firm ass as she bent over.

"Trust me, when it comes to women like you, all men are like that."

She raised her eyebrows. "Oh, yeah? Even you?"

"*Especially* me."

A sizzle of tension rolled down my spine. Damn it all if I could figure out how she even made her lime-green zoo polo look like the sexiest thing in the world. Her pretty golden hair was pulled back in a ponytail, emphasizing the crystal clearness of those bright eyes, but when I spoke, she looked away from me, focusing instead on the baby in her arms.

Which, of course, made her look all the more irresistible.

As she stared down at the little lump in the pen, she practically glowed, and when she smiled, it seemed like she was grinning with all of her body. Like she was truly, blissfully happy. Like she loved her job more than life itself.

And that was a feeling I knew all too well. But even more than that, I couldn't escape the very real feeling that she would be just as enamored of our own baby…if we were having one, that was.

Bren cleared her throat, pulling us both from the tense moment my reply had created. "Tell me, Mr. Baby Expert, have you ever fed a baby pig?"

I cocked an eyebrow. "Can't say that I have."

"Then I think it's time you learned." She motioned for me to join her and I followed her instructions, standing so close that our skin brushed as I reached for one of the pig's siblings. "This little guys is special."

"I thought you weren't supposed to have favorites."

"Oh, I have favorites in every enclosure. Like the new koala baby's mom, Sheila. I love her."

"And what makes a koala so special?"

She shrugged a single shoulder. "She just is. She has the most personality of any of the other koalas, which is why all the males try to imprint on her."

"Imprint?"

She laughed. "You really don't know much about animals, huh?"

"Clearly."

"When a koala wants to mate with another koala, he excretes a certain pheromone from his chest and rubs it on his intended."

"And they say romance is dead?" I murmured, a grin hitching my lips. I always enjoyed my work, but I couldn't deny, being here with her had been the highlight of my day so far.

Bren rolled her eyes. "Sheila is the belle of the ball in the koala habitat."

I nodded. "So, what's your favorite animal?"

"Type or in particular?"

I laughed. "How about both?"

"Personally, I'm a big fan of Nibs, the cheetah. But I also like caring for the babies…"

"Why can't the piglets mother feed them?"

Her gaze turned soft and her thoughts looked faraway. "She got an infection in her milk ducts shortly after delivering. Poor thing is on some strong antibiotics and needs her rest so she can recover."

"I can see why you like them so much," I said, still marveling at how cute the damn things were routing around in the hay, and mewling softly as they got cozy.

Bren nodded. "They're sweet."

"Like you," I said, and a slow pink flush took over her cheeks.

When it's bottle was done, she took the pig from my arms, settled the animal back in its pen, and then locked up the gate before leading me down the pathway.

"So, look, I don't know if you had plans tonight, but I've got a ton of food in my fridge and nobody to share it with. Interested in coming over tonight and letting me cook for you?" I asked, trying to keep it nonchalant even though my blood pulsed through my body in hot rushes.

She studied my face for a long moment, apparently considering her options.

"I won't try anything funny," I said, then added, "unless, of course, you want me to."

"Let's see how it goes."

"Is that a yes?" I asked.

"Yeah, why not. Let's have dinner." She turned and led me out of the enclosure, careful to make sure I sanitized my hands again on the way out, but I was only half listening to her instructions.

I'd reverted back into my head, busy planning what I would cook for her—what I would say next.

What I was going to do to replay that incredible night we'd shared so many weeks before.

Because today had only sealed the deal for me.

If I had any say in the matter, Bren Matthews was going to end this night screaming my name and begging me for more.

Chapter Thirteen

Bren

"This is it. Which I guess you know."

Mason opened the door to his apartment, and again I was greeted by the cool, modern lines of his penthouse suite that I was sure I'd never see again. The glass wall along the back of the room framed the fading sunset and the outline of the city, and as he flicked on the lights, I was blown away by the crisp, sharp lines of his cream-and-slate-gray furniture.

After we'd left the zoo, I'd gone home after work for a quick shower and changed into a gauzy sundress in pale peach. Based on Mason's lingering perusal, he approved of my wardrobe change.

I slipped off my sandals and then padded toward the kitchen, trying to beat back the memory of the last time I'd been here, half-naked and searching for my clothes, but I couldn't help it. Internally I cringed at my former self, the guilt of having slunk out like a coward sinking in the more I got to know him.

"The place is beautiful," I said, though inside I began to wonder where—in all the glass coffee tables and chrome fixtures—a baby might fit in. Maybe a stainless-steel crib to match the decor?

But we weren't thinking about babies. We were thinking about…what?

Ever since I'd thought there was a possibility of this baby, I'd hardly been able to think of anything else. And now, faced with the prospect of having to talk, I wasn't sure I had a word left to say that wasn't about custody or how I wanted our potential child to be raised.

"Thanks," he said, and for a moment I'd forgotten what he was thanking me for. The apartment, right. I'd said he had a nice apartment.

He followed me into the kitchen after slipping off his own shoes, then opened the fridge door and pulled out a bottle of water. "Thirsty?"

I shook my head.

He closed the door and leaned back against it. "Is everything okay? You're quiet."

"Yeah." I swallowed. "Just not sure what to say."

"Then let me guide you." He smiled warmly, sending a shiver of awareness through me. "First, tell me what you want to eat that isn't soft cheese, sushi, or alcohol-related?"

I laughed despite myself. "Well, uh, I don't know what you have."

He shrugged. "I can make you anything. There's steak and the makings of tortillas. Quesadillas? Fajitas? Pasta? Or there's chicken if you're less into red meat."

"Steak sounds good." I gave him another nervous nod and he pulled the package from the fridge—a rectangular container with two massive porterhouse steaks inside.

"You were going to make fajitas with a porterhouse?" I asked.

He grabbed a frying pan hanging from the rack over the island and shrugged. "I was going to make you whatever you wanted. Now tell me, what do you like with your steak?"

"More steak?" I said, and he laughed.

"You got it." He grabbed a bag of slivered almonds from a nearby cabinet, then moved back to the

The Soul Mate

fridge for some green beans. I watched as he moved quietly and quickly, never consulting a cookbook.

"You actually cook," I said, recognizing his total comfort in the kitchen with a start. Was there anything this man couldn't do?

He nodded. "I do. When my mom was sick, my dad did the cooking and he was god-awful. I figured someone had to figure out how to make edible food or we would all waste away even if she beat the cancer."

I smiled. The story was a familiar one—it was the same thing I'd done when my father had passed away. Of course, I'd been only twelve back then, but with my father gone, my mother hardly ever remembered to eat, let alone to feed me.

I'd never gotten good enough to make anything fancy without a recipe, but I knew my way around a gas range, which was still more than I could ever say for my mom.

"What are you thinking about?" he asked, his deep voice breaking through my thoughts.

"Nothing. Well, I was thinking I should help you. And that it must have been hard, watching your mom so sick like that." No point in mentioning that I could empathize from experience. I still didn't know how close I really wanted to get with Mason. I barely knew him, even if our DNA were friends.

"We all have our trials," he said, deftly moving the indigents around before he reached for another pan. "And you stay exactly where you are. I don't want you lifting a finger."

"I could get used to that," I said with a chuckle.

But you better not get used to it, Bren Matthews. Because if you do, you'll find yourself flying straight out of the frying pan and into the fire.

He smiled back at me, then focused in on his work again, heating the pans and sautéing the almonds while I imagined myself falling so far and so deep I wouldn't know where I ended and he began. No. Not gonna happen. "You know, you'd think that it would have been a huge toll on them, what happened with my mom, but my parents really made the best of it. Every day we did something together as a family. I mean, I know now that was because we didn't know how many days my mom might have left, but then?" He shrugged a shoulder, then moved back to the fridge for a forgotten ingredient. "It was just, I don't know, good. To see my parents together and happy together in spite of everything. It makes you feel like anything is possible, seeing two people like that."

"I know what you mean." I'd said the words without thinking—or rather, without realizing what I'd done. I didn't want to open the door to my past. Not yet. Maybe not ever.

Of course, he would have to meet my mother eventually, and when he did, the whole sordid affair would come out—how happy my life had been when my parents had been together. And how completely and totally inconsolable she had been since my dad's passing.

My throat tightened, and I cleared it as I watched him move around the kitchen. Mason went right back to preparing dinner and didn't seem to notice all the words that remained unsaid.

He tossed two cloves of garlic and a bundle of thyme into the heating pan, and a savory, mouthwatering aroma filled the air.

"Anyway," he said. "I feel like I talk all the time about myself and I don't know enough about you."

I blinked. "Well, what do you want to know?"

"Anything, anything at all. Like, why do you go by your middle name?"

"My middle name is Brennan, but I prefer Bren," I said.

"That's cool." He nodded. "Why did your parents name you Ashley?"

I rolled my eyes. "The stupidest reason you can imagine."

"You have to remember I've seen a lot of people name babies stupid things for stupid reasons. Ashley hardly seems far out there."

"Right," I said. "Well, my mom and dad met at an old-timey sort of movie theater and it was playing *Gone With the Wind* that night. So, you know, my mom named me Ashley because she fell in love with that character."

"That's not stupid. That's actually very sweet." The steak sizzled in the pan behind him and he turned around to tend the meat. "Ashley was a middle name, too. It could have been worse, because they could have used his first name and called you George."

I snorted and leaned back in my chair. "I like Bren a lot better. It's a family name. My grandma was Bren, too."

He nodded. "Family connections are important. But it's nice to have a love story in your name. Like a little reminder."

All the more reason to go by Bren, I thought. Every sorrowful lilt of my mother's voice was reminder enough of my parent's tragedy of a love story—I didn't need to add my name to the list.

"Are your parents still together?" he asked.

A knife dug between my ribs, and I chewed on the inside of my cheek, wondering how best to answer him. I wasn't about to lie to him—but I didn't need to say all of it either. Not now. Not yet. Maybe not ever.

"No," I said simply.

He nodded, and silence fell between us for a long moment before he slid a plate—steamy and hot—in front of me. On it was a massive serving of porterhouse and green beans amandine.

"Wow, this looks incredible," I said, then waited as he slid a knife and fork toward me and then joined me at the island to eat.

"Your steak is smaller than mine," I said. "Let's swap."

"You said you like your steak with more steak, and you might be eating for two."

"And if I'm not?" I said.

"Then you still get more steak. Seems like a win-win to me." He cut into his steak, then said, "Shit, I forgot to ask—are you okay with medium?"

"Perfect," I said, then started in on my food. With every bite, I was more amazed with his prowess in the kitchen, and I was on the point of telling him as much when he started to speak again.

"Your job is amazing," he said. "Watching what you do." He shook his head. "I'm impressed."

"Well, I don't save lives or anything."

"I'll bet you do," he countered. "Animals need to be cared for just as much as humans."

The Soul Mate   127

My heart melted a little, and I swallowed hard, trying not to get sucked in to the whirling, twirling human vortex of perfection that was Mason Bentley.

"Anyway, what else do you want to know about me?" I asked.

"What was your favorite toy when you were a kid?"

"What?" I laughed.

"I'm serious. You can tell a lot about a person based on their favorite childhood toy."

"Even if it was just a doll?" I raised my eyebrows, then took another bite of my green beans.

"What kind of doll?"

"A veterinarian doll set I got for my seventh birthday." It had been a special gift from my father. He'd run all through all the surrounding cities trying to find one just for me. That was just the kind of guy he'd been.

"What was her name?"

I blushed. "Oh God."

"Come on," he coaxed.

"Valerie Veterinarian."

"You still have her?" he asked.

"No." I shook my head. "Lost her in a move. But what about you? Favorite childhood toy?"

"Too many to name."

"Ah, so you were spoiled," I teased.

"I was well-loved," he amended with a wide grin.

"I see." I nodded. "Well, gun to your head, what was your favorite?"

"I don't know. I guess…I had a stuffed giraffe when I was little. I mean, really little. There are a bunch of pictures of me with it."

"What was his name?" I asked.

He shrugged. "We had no need for names. Our connection was more spiritual than that."

I laughed out loud. "Right. Well, good to know."

We finished our meal and before I got the chance to clean up, Mason grabbed my dish and handled everything for me. Which left me to sit there, wondering what came next. Our conversation was a little awkward,

The Soul Mate 129

but that was to be expected. We were still in the getting-to-know-you stage. But he was trying—cooking for me, asking questions about me, and attempting to make me feel comfortable. He was one of the good guys—and that's what scared me.

I couldn't very well eat and run.

Worse, I didn't want to.

I wanted to run, all right. Run straight into his bedroom and thank him for dinner in the most intimate way I could. But then, of course, that was only because I knew this time could never be as good as the last.

If I slept with him tonight—which I definitely wasn't going to—but if I *did*? Maybe I'd finally have a lukewarm memory to wash away the searing hotness of our first night together. There was no way it could be as good as I remembered. No way.

Or at least, that's what I kept telling myself as I tried to justify still wanting to sleep with him.

Which I *totally* wasn't going to do.

"Want to watch a little TV?" Mason asked as he stepped away from the sink, rolling his thick shoulders to stretch and leaving me with my tongue hanging out.

"TV sounds good," I said, wondering if I should plant the seed for my early departure now so it would be an easy, hassle-free extraction.

"Cool. Pick your poison." He turned on the flat-screen TV hanging on the wall opposite his bedroom, his Netflix cue already loaded.

"Lots of car shows." I nodded toward the screen.

"Yeah." He shoved his hands in his pockets, then settled back onto his cream-colored sofa. "I've got one I'm working on. Probably not worth the price I pay to store it, but it's a hobby."

"What kind of car is it?"

"A Mustang," he said. "My dad taught me how to work on old muscle cars when I was growing up. It helps to have something to do with your hands or to unwind after a bad day."

I could think of something he could do to occupy his hands. Shaking the mental image away of his weight pinning me to the bed while I moaned, I moved toward the sofa.

"I can understand that," I said.

In fact, the similarities in our lives growing up were almost eerily similar. Before my father had gotten sick, I spent almost every Saturday in our garage, watching him as he toiled over a Cadillac he'd inherited from my grandfather. He used to tell me that oil ran in our blood and that—once I figured out my true calling—there'd finally be a mechanic in the family.

Every time I'd laugh and he'd explain that he was kidding, but that if I ever wanted to work on the car I could join him. Instead, I'd always sat on my stool and handed him tools as he fiddled with this or that and tried to explain to me what he was doing. I never understood, of course. I was too young then.

But selling that Cadillac once he was gone to help my mom get on her feet financially? That had been one of the hardest days of my life. Handing over the keys had been like handing over a part of my dad to some random stranger.

"Maybe not car stuff," I said. "You ever watch *Jane the Virgin*? That's a pretty funny show."

"No, what's it about?"

"It's about a girl who accidentally gets pregnant and—" I heard myself, then stopped. "You know what? That one is probably a bad idea too."

He laughed. "Maybe we should just talk." He patted the seat beside him on the sofa, and I could feel his gaze raking over me, surveying me. He knew, of course, what was underneath my clothes. He'd already seen me—all of me.

So why did I still feel so exposed? Because baring my body was far easier than stripping away the curtain to my soul.

Joining him on the couch, I crossed my legs if only to dull the ache that rose inside me at the smell of his spicy-sweet cologne. "What do you want to talk about now?" I asked.

"You. Always you," he said.

I grabbed a nearby throw pillow and hugged it close. "Well, not much to say there. You know where I work and my favorite childhood toy. That's about all of it."

He laughed, then moved a little closer, so close that his arm brushed against mine. "Do you date much? Any serious relationships you want to rehash? Bad blind dates, maybe? Tinder horror stories?"

"Well…" I thought hard about my answer. What I did technically couldn't be called dating. Unless, of course, he counted my long-term, committed relationship with my friendly bedside vibrator. If that were the case, I'd bet at this point I could petition for common law marriage.

"Not quite," I said.

"So before me, the last guy was?"

"Years ago," I confessed, averting my gaze.

"I wondered," he murmured.

"Something about me just screams cat lady?" I joked.

"No." He shook his head. "You were…I could tell."

"How could you tell?" I narrowed my eyes, wondering what in the hell he meant. That I was so inexperienced and rusty it gave me away? White hot annoyance crept up my spine and landed on the back of my neck. Maybe I'd just discovered a minor flaw marring his perfect resume.

"Honestly? You were just so tight," he said, his voice dropping lower. "I've been wondering ever since then if it was because you hadn't been with anyone for a while, or if maybe you always feel that way. So wet and warm and—"

There was no denying the surge of need building between my thighs now, and my breath caught as I met his gaze. "I-I don't know."

His eyes went dark and his jaw tensed.

"Only one way to find out," he said.

Chapter Fourteen

Bren

I should have said no.

I will be the first person to admit that, when propositioned by my potential baby daddy, the answer should have been unequivocal and sure.

No.

No thank you.

Not again.

But that answer, of course, didn't factor in the way he looked at me—the way his blue eyes raked over my skin like he was touching it already, laving it with his tongue and readying me for his thick, hard cock.

I licked my bottom lip, trying to work up the discipline to stop this freight train of lust before it left the station. Still, if I slept with him again, maybe it really would put all my worries to rest. That night could have been amazing simply because it had been so long for me.

What could it hurt to put my assumptions to rest? Yeah, right. It could hurt *me*.

Now, after I'd already been sated by him once, there was no way his body could have the same effect. No, this time would be a tepid bath compared to the hot, steamy whirlpool that the last time had been.

Which meant giving it a try could only be a good thing.

I struggled to breathe in the heavy silence, and then Mason finally spoke.

"Let's take things slow. We won't do anything you're not ready for."

I nodded. Slow. That was a good idea. And one I could get behind.

He inched closer on the couch, lowering his mouth toward my neck.

"Just want to touch you," he murmured. His full lips brushed my collarbone, making me shiver.

Trailing soft kisses up my neck, my jawline, Mason finally brought his mouth to mine.

Our lips met in a hungry kiss, our bodies remembering every touch, every breath with perfect clarity.

"No pressure, okay?" Mason whispered, encouragingly against my lips.

I nodded, gripping the back of his neck to draw him in for another kiss.

Soon his hand slid up my thigh, only stopping when he brushed the front of my panties. My knees parted for him on instinct.

He stroked the front of my dampened panties, finding the spot that made me squirm.

"More," I groaned.

"I knew I liked you," he chuckled against my mouth.

Slipping his fingers beneath the fabric, Mason penetrated me, slowly.

"You're not tender, are you?" he whispered.

"Damn it, Mason. Don't treat me like I'm…"

"Pregnant?" he supplied.

My answering frown implored him in a wordless request not to destroy the mood.

"Duly noted."

Adding a second finger, he pressed deeper, making me cry out. Damn, the man was skilled, but something gnawed at the back of my brain. I wanted this, I did, it was just that…if we weren't careful, I could easily see myself losing my head. And what if I *wasn't* pregnant? This is exactly what had gotten me into this pickle in the first place.

"Wait, wait, wait," I mumbled, pulling back to put several inches of space between us. "This isn't slow."

"Fuck." He scrubbed a hand through his hair. "No, I guess it's not."

Mason looked down at my swollen lips, touching me there with his fingertips. "How's this? No sex. But we both get to come."

I was nodding before my brain even processed my agreement. "I like how you compromise." I liked a lot of things about him, I was finding out. But in my heart, I already knew. Because if I didn't really like him, I wouldn't want to run away from him every time a new wave of unwelcome emotion flowed over me.

He lifted my calf, planting my foot beside me on the couch so that my legs were open for him. "Don't move. I want you just like this." Slipping his fingers past the edge of my panties, he stroked just where I needed him. My entire body clenched and squeezed, wanting so much more, but already dangerously close to falling over the edge.

Mason brought his mouth to mine once again, kissing me deeply while his fingers did very naughty things.

I struggled to get his pants open, fumbling with the button. When he knocked my hands away, I couldn't help the soft, happy noise that escaped me.

He freed himself, stroking once. The bead of moisture at his tip distracted me in the most wonderful way.

"You going to look at it all night, or are you going to touch me?" he groaned.

Taking my hand in his, he guided it to his cock.

I took him into my hand and stroked gently at first, then harder. He dropped his head back against the couch and allowed me to have my way with him, every now and then letting out a little grunt of approval.

I'd thought that first night he seemed so big only because it had been so long since I'd been with someone—and even longer since I'd wanted someone so much. Now, though? Looking at him again? I knew I'd been wrong. He was thick and long and throbbing for me.

"Need you to touch me," I moaned.

"Fuck yes."

His fingers were back at work, and within moments I was writhing beneath his touch.

"Going to come," I murmured.

"Not yet you're not." He slowed his pace, teasing my swollen flesh as I rocked my hips into his touch, vying for more attention. "Together," he whispered, kissing my lips again. "Grip me a little tighter."

I obeyed.

"That's it," he grunted. "*Fuck.*"

He was so sexy like this, so masculine. I loved how bossy he was during sex. How vocal.

Still kissing me, Mason returned his attention to my lady bits, making white light spark behind my eyelids.

"I'm so close," I whispered against the onslaught of his kisses.

"Take your time. I'm in no rush."

I'd forgotten that about him—his stamina…and a delicious flashback of our night together ripped through my brain.

"Mace…"

"That's it. Come for me. I'm right behind you."

I pumped my hand firmly up and down, my climax crashing through me just as I felt his hot, sticky release. *Together.*

Remembering our night together, I realized again how uncanny it was how in sync we were. This wasn't normal, was it?

Pulling his T-shirt off over his head, Mason balled it up and used it to wipe the semen off my hand, and then his rock-hard abs.

What kind of man cooked a perfect steak, delivered prenatal vitamins to you at work, and then brought you to orgasm in five minutes flat?

Chapter Fifteen

Bren

What had just happened... What was everything I had just felt? It was too much, too fast. Overwhelming and scary and real and if I didn't get away soon, it would only get worse. White-hot panic enveloped me, creeping into every single cell in my body. It screamed for attention.

I had to get out of here.

With every breath, every beat of my heart, I knew it.

My heart was still hammering wildly as I pulled away, trying not to make eye contact with Mason as he wiped me clean. He ran a possessive hand over my belly as I sat up, his eyes lingering there as he studied me.

As I stood, Mason fastened his pants again and then paused, shooting me a questioning glance.

"I'm going to get changed and we can decide what to do for the rest of the night," he called over his shoulder, his gaze raking over my body and sending a shiver through me.

Slowly I trailed behind him, trying to come up with some excuse for why I couldn't stay. I didn't have a dog or cat to feed and no roommate was waiting for me at home. I didn't have to work the next day. Still, I didn't think "I'm a big fat chicken" felt like a valid excuse, and it certainly wasn't one I wanted to utter out loud. This whole damn situation defied logic so I couldn't justify my behavior. I wanted to run. Period.

With a deep breath, I followed him into the bedroom and watched as he pulled on a hoodie and pajama pants, then tossed a T-shirt and pants onto his gray comforter.

He nodded toward the clothes. "For you. If you want to get more comfortable."

I forced a smile. "No thanks. I think I'm going to get going."

His gaze narrowed on my face and it was all I could do not to squirm. Even though he didn't say anything, his expression said it all.

Coward.

"What's the rush?" he asked softly.

You just knocked my socks off again and that wasn't supposed to be how it went. You can own my body but you can't own my heart.

But I couldn't say that either.

"You should stay. We'll go into the living room and watch some TV."

I shook my head, panic ceasing my heartbeat in my chest. "I don't think so."

"Something better to do, or just need some space?" he asked as he picked up a pile of socks and shoved them into a new drawer before turning to face me. It was freakish how well he knew me after so short a time. He was getting close to figuring me out. Too close.

"What are you doing?" I asked, my voice going shrill.

"Making room for you. My place is closer to the zoo than yours, and that way, if there is a night you *do* decide to stay, it will be easy. You can keep some clothes here and—"

"What? No." I blinked. "We barely know each other, Mason."

He closed the drawer before turning to face me and crossing his arms over his chest. "We know that we fit together like hand in glove," he said, his eyes skimming over me and making me shiver. "We know that I might be the father of your child. And we know that we like each other's company. It only makes sense that we try to spend some time together so that we can get to know each other even better, doesn't it? Isn't that what we agreed to do?"

"No, it doesn't make sense, and no, that wasn't what we agreed to do," I shot back. "None of this makes sense. Look, what we just did? That was a mistake. I should have gone before. Just pretend it never happened, okay? I don't know what I was thinking."

"You were thinking you're attracted to me. Just like I'm attracted to you. I thought we established that." He took another step toward me, but I retreated, making my way toward the bedroom door.

"I need to get some air. Some time to think. I'll call you…or something."

I sprinted for my sandals and slid them on quickly before heading for the front door. When my hand closed around the knob, I felt a warm, masculine hand on my bicep, but I yanked my shoulder away and hurried out the door without bothering to turn around.

That orgasm?

My own drawer?

Oh, hell no.

It was all too much. He was too much, and I had to get out of there before this thing between us swallowed me whole.

Chapter Sixteen

Mason

I got as far as the hall outside my apartment, watching her almost insane mad dash to the elevators, when the phone in my pocket vibrated.

At first, I thought it might be better to ignore it—to follow Bren down to the lobby and walk her to her car at the very least, but after what just happened, there was no doubting that she needed space and I had no choice but to give it to her. Even though I didn't work at the zoo like she did, I knew what happened when you tried to cage a wild animal.

The only question was why she needed space to begin with.

After everything that had happened today—the zoo, dinner, and the mind-blowing almost-sex—I thought we were finally making progress. But she felt different...

I heard the distant ding of the elevator doors, then headed back inside my apartment, and my phone buzzed again against my thigh.

Gritting my teeth, I fished the device from my pocket and swiped my thumb across the glass to see that I had missed a call from my mother and she'd left a message.

I thumbed the voice mail button and pressed the smartphone to my ear, listening as the warm, familiar tone of my mother's voice floated through the speaker.

"Mason, honey, it's mom. I was calling to ask if you might be able to come over tonight or tomorrow? Your father and I have something important to tell you and we'd like if you could stop by the house so we can do it in person."

My heart jumped into my throat as the recording ended.

Something important to tell me? The last time I'd gotten a call like this, I'd been on my way to Johns Hopkins, ready to start my freshman year and make a name for myself, only to turn around and find that the world was coming apart. My mother was sick with cancer. Potentially terminal.

The idea of a recurrence hadn't been far from my mind ever since. It was the reason I'd never moved away and tried to make sure I always made time with both my parents, no matter how busy life got. And if my mom was sick again…

My stomach tightened at the thought.

I'd been on top of the world only ten minutes before, with Bren's warm, solid palm pressed against my cock, and now my whole life had turned into one giant shit show.

I shot a quick text to my mom and slipped into a pair of shoes before locking my apartment and heading for the parking garage. If my parents needed to tell me something, then I was going to be there to hear it—come hell or high water.

I broke nearly every traffic law on the books trying to get there, but when I finally pulled up in front of the classic brick house where I'd grown up, I felt worse instead of better. It just all felt so familiar—the call, the drive, all of it. And when I went inside, I felt intense dread, like I already knew what would be waiting for me on the other end.

Steeling myself, I rapped on the door once before letting myself in with my spare key. My mother appeared on the other side of the door just as I stepped in, her blue eyes wary as she looked me over.

"You got here awfully fast."

"If there's something you couldn't tell me on the phone, I wanted to know what it was right away."

She nodded, pursing her lips. "I can understand that. Come in. Your father just made coffee."

The tension around her eyes and the fact that she didn't elaborate then or there settled it. My gut clenched and I braced myself for the blow.

Jesus, what if this was it? If she was sick again and Bren was pregnant, it would add a whole new level of grief to the mix. She wanted grandchildren so desperately.

Full of dread, I followed her into the quaint living room and settled onto one of the pink floral couches as my father appeared in the doorway with a black coffee carafe in his hand and a tray of mugs in the other.

"Let me help you with that." My mother rushed toward him and took the tray, setting it on the coffee table between us before taking a seat opposite me and beside my father.

For a moment, silence fell over us and my father leaned forward, the light shining off his bald spot, as he poured three cups of black coffee and handed one to my mother and one to me.

"So let's hear it. What going on?" I asked.

My parents looked at one another, then back at me.

Finally my mother cleared her throat. "Your father and I have come to an important decision, and we felt it was important that you knew about it as soon as we were certain."

"Okay." I nodded, my skull pounding with a tension headache as I resisted the urge to demand they just say it already.

"We've decided that, as we are now entering new stages in our lives, we'd be better off apart from one another," my father said, patting my mother on her knee as she nodded solemnly.

I examined each of them, not sure I'd heard them right. Apart from one another?

"What does that mean, exactly?"

"We mean we're going to enter into a trial separation," my mother said, the finality in her voice ringing through the otherwise silent room.

For the next minute, my brain did a decathlon. On one hand, I felt nothing but relief. Neither of them was dying or prepping to spend months in the hospital dripping poison into their veins to kill something worse than poison. On the other, this was the second thing that had happened in the past hour that made absolutely no sense.

"I don't understand. You guys have always been inseparable." I shot a pointed gaze at the spot where my father's hand rested on my mother's knee. "Even now, you're a team."

My dad pulled his hand away and sighed.

"Just because we're separating doesn't mean we don't love and support one another. And I know it probably feels like we have a perfect marriage because we're your parents and we don't fight, but if you really think about it, do you think that's true?" my mother asked. "Do you think we're a good match?"

I took a deep breath, thinking her words over carefully. In truth, I knew they had their differences—every couple did. My mother had always been the life of the party, the light in every room she entered. Whenever I called her, she was on her way to some bingo tournament or garden luncheon while my father stayed home, desperate to find out what happened on the next episode of one crime drama or another, and was happiest with his nose buried in a book.

Sure, they had different interests, but was that really reason enough for a divorce?

"Our differences are significant," my father cut in. "Your mother wants to go and explore the world and now that we're getting older, I can't bring myself to hold her back. But I also can't bring myself to even think about traveling like that."

"We are still a family." My mother smiled from my father to me. "We always will be. We have shared so much of our lives with one another and we have you, but I can't sit around this house and become an old lady who knits and stares out the window, wishing for more."

"And I wouldn't want you to." My father nodded toward her, then closed his hand over hers. He shot a glance to me and shrugged. "It's time, son. And we are both at peace with it."

My mouth went completely dry. Were they serious right now? It'd be one thing if they'd been unhappy. I'd be fully supportive, encouraging each of them to move on to something that made them happier. But this? What in the what? I took a deep breath, searching for the words I knew I was supposed to say as their adult son.

"You should do whatever makes you both happiest, of course. It's a shock, is all, so I'm just trying to process." Now that I'd finally found my voice, I couldn't seem to shut up. "I thought you guys had this fairy-tale marriage, you know?"

"A lot of kids think that," Mom said. "You never would have known the struggle and compromises we've made along the way to make it work as long as it did."

"But the cancer—"

"—was terrible," Dad said with a wince, his eyes soft with remembered pain. "But just because someone stood by you through a bad time doesn't mean you're shackled to him for life. We get only so much time and we each should guard it as we get older. Use it exactly as we each see fit."

"Exactly. So instead of ignoring the fact that we are different people, we've decided to embrace it and try to find our bliss while we still can." My mother squeezed my father's hand. "We hope once you've wrapped your head around it all, you can understand and support that decision."

I nodded slowly and then pushed myself to my feet.

"I need to get some air. Are you guys okay if I just take a little walk and come back in ten?" I asked.

I was a grown-ass man and my parents had to live their lives. There was no question I would support and love them unconditionally. But suddenly, the room felt stuffy and hot and I had to get out, if only to reconcile everything that had just happened.

"Sure thing, sweetie," Mom said, but I was already halfway toward the door, ready to breathe in the crisp evening air and think through…well, my entire life, really.

Every decision I'd made, every relationship I'd been in had been founded on the belief that once you found your soul mate, that was it. Game over. You stayed together through thick and thin. There was no challenge or difference too great for the two of you to overcome.

Now, though? That was gone. And the timing couldn't have been worse, from a totally selfish standpoint. I was on the precipice of a huge relationship in my own life with someone who was gun-shy and possibly pregnant with my child. Not only that, I was locked and loaded to go all in based on my own confidence in the premise of soul mates and my unshakeable belief that I'd found mine.

Only soul mates weren't real. Or at least, the pair I'd always hung my hat on weren't. And I couldn't deny, this news was like an A-bomb, obliterating my world and shaking one of my core beliefs.

I took the familiar route I used to walk when I'd hung around with my friends in this neighborhood, but I barely noticed the brick homes or stately trees as I strode past them. Instead, I was focused on my life, the faces of all the girls I'd run through or disappointed over the years because I'd had such strict blinders on. I'd been searching for my one and only the entire time.

If my parents' happy, perfect relationship wasn't as happy or perfect as I'd thought, then why had I stayed single for so long? Why had I insisted on being so choosy about the person I'd finally settle down with?

Not for the first time, I thought about fate. That maybe, after all of this, fate had forced me to be single in the hope that it would lead me to Bren and, maybe, our baby?

But now, if my parents were right, what did any of it matter? I had only the here and now.

For the next ten minutes, I ate up the block with my stride, trying to work off some of the tension that had been building since Bren had left.

By the time I got back to my parents' house, I was feeling less breathless and my brain had finally calmed.

My parents were healthy and, by the looks of it, happy with their decision. They would be fine and so would I. And as for Bren?

Nothing had changed for me.

I thought of her panicked face as she'd sprinted from my apartment. Of her sweet-smelling hair and her soft lips. Of the way her mouth tilted to the side when there was something else on her mind—something she wouldn't, or maybe couldn't, tell me. She was hiding something, and I just hoped she'd tell me before it was too late.

She was like no other woman I'd ever known and if it wasn't love yet, I was well on my way. She could say what she wanted but her body didn't lie. She was just as into me as I was into her. She was just scared.

I'd known that from the beginning and I'd pushed too hard. She needed time. Time I hadn't been giving her.

The drawer had been a stupid idea, but I could make it up to her. I just had to figure out how, and how the fuck to get a hold of some extra patience.

Because I had a feeling I was going to need it. Even if soul mates were a crock of shit, she and I needed our shot.

Chapter Seventeen

Bren

"Guess who brought donuts."

Mandy's chipper singsong echoed through the front hall of my apartment and I grimaced, groaning to let her know where I was before shoving my pillow over my face.

Lord knew I wasn't in shape for company—I was barely in shape to be around myself.

Ever since I'd left Mason's last night, I hadn't been able to think about anything other than what a complete and total ass I'd been and the sheer, utter terror that had filled my heart as soon as I'd realized what our hot, passionate moment of fun had become.

Together.

Not that Mandy would understand.

In her mind, everything was rainbows and puppy dogs and every chance at love ought to be snatched up and savored—at least, that was the only way I could figure she'd gotten married so young. But that was just it. She was married. She didn't know, couldn't know, what a risk it was to take a chance on someone nowadays. It was a jungle out here.

A gentle knock sounded on my wooden bedroom door and I croaked for her to come in, though I didn't bother to drag the pillow from over my face. Distantly, I heard the rustle of her donut bag and caught the savory, sweet smell of my favorite hazelnut latte.

"If that's what I think it is, you're a goddess," I muttered.

"Good morning, Sleeping Beauty." There was a little thunk and I peeked through the small space between my comforter and pillow to see her setting a tray of drinks on my nightstand before she poked me in the stomach. "It's ten thirty," she said with a disapproving click of her tongue.

"So?" I grumbled. "It's Sunday."

"Which means you should already have gone on your run and come back by now."

"I can't run. I'm pregnant," I argued.

"You don't know that," she shot back with a chuckle. "And besides, I'm pretty sure pregnant people are allowed to run."

"It'll wiggle the baby. Or something," I said stubbornly, pushing the covers off me. Any excuse not to run was just fine by me.

"If your new boyfriend taught you that, then I have some bad news about his credentials as a doctor. Now come on, get up and have a donut with me."

Grumbling to myself, I propped a few pillows between my back and the headboard, then grabbed for the cup with my name on it.

"Is this caffeine-free?" I asked suspiciously.

"Yup." Mandy nodded. "Who knows? The caffeine might—what was the medical term you used? Ah, yes. It might 'wiggle the baby.' We'd hate to have that happen." She rolled her eyes, then took her own cup from the cardboard carrier and brought it to her lips.

I took a sip of hazelnut goodness, sighing at the comforting heat before meeting my friend's questioning gaze.

"So, spill. What's the real reason you're still in bed?" she asked.

"Jeez, can't a girl sleep in every now and then?" I muttered.

"A girl can. Just not you." Mandy raised her eyebrows. "You didn't have morning sickness or anything, right?"

I shook my head. "No, no. Nothing like that. I've just got a lot on my mind, that's all."

"Mason stuff?" Mandy pressed.

"Wow, three seconds after I wake up and I'm already being interrogated." She waited expectantly and I knew she wasn't going to get off my back unless I told her, so finally I blurted, "Fine, yes, if you must know. Mason stuff."

"What happened? He confessed his love?" Mandy asked, taking another nonchalant sip of her coffee.

"What? No." My cheeks flamed as renewed terror consumed me. "God, what would make you say that?"

"Because that's always when I find you in bed like this," Mandy shot back.

"I've never done this before," I said, taking another sip from my cup and glaring at her.

"Haven't you?" she sniffed. "What about two years ago with that Venezuelan guy…what was his name? Don?"

I rolled my eyes again. "That was nothing. He moved way too fast. Buying me a new computer for my birthday? Who did he think he was, fucking Christian Grey, for crying out loud? Take it easy, am I right?" I asked with a snort.

Mandy frowned. "And Devon from work?"

"That wasn't even a thing," I protested. "We went on three dates."

"Until he told you how gorgeous you were in the moonlight and you wigged out and told him you never wanted to see him again."

"What?" I scowled at her through narrowed eyes. "Who told you that?" I recalled specifically not detailing that little breakup to her because I knew she'd judge me over it.

Maybe because you deserve her judgment? a little voice in my head whispered. I wanted to fire that damn voice of reason and tell it to get lost.

"He did," Mandy said. "I was waiting for you to finish your evening rounds and he was on his way out. He stopped and asked me what he'd done to turn you into a psycho."

A psycho?

Ouch.

"And what did you tell him?" I asked, my stomach feeling queasy.

"That you have a habit of picking guys you can't get emotionally attached to and he shouldn't take it personally. You're just broken inside." She shrugged as if spilling my personal dirt to the world meant nothing.

"Jesus, Mandy. Tell me how you really feel."

"I always do. That's why you keep me around," she said with a smug smile. "Don't get me wrong, though. I still love you."

"Good, because you're wrong," I said.

She laughed. "Is that so? So, you're going to tell me the Mason thing that has you lying in bed like an invalid has nothing to do with the fact that you maybe actually like him and he tried to get close to you?"

"I let him get close to me," I said. "We…did some stuff that was—"

Scary.

"Romantic," I finished.

"Okay, so did he then introduce you to his toenail collection? Or punch you in the face?"

"Well, no…"

"Did he drop to one knee and ask you to marry him? Because that might be rushing things and that I could see," she said, taking a big bite of a chocolate glazed donut and chewing while she waited for my response.

"Not exactly." But it was close. "He offered me a drawer."

"A drawer?"

"Yeah, you know, like to leave stuff at his place or whatever," I said, trying not to fidget as she stared me down.

"Oh my God. Did you call the police? Get a restraining order?" she demanded, eyes wide in faux shock.

"Okay, okay, I hear it now as I say it out loud. Not that big of a deal," I admitted, which sent her off into a fit of laughter.

"Not a big deal at all. Especially since you agreed to spend some time with him and slept with him. Which only goes to prove my point that you have commitment issues. After all, you're lying in your own bed instead of his right now."

"It's complicated," I tried again.

"It's not. You like him but you're doing what you always do. You know, I've been handling this with kid gloves for a long time now, but considering everything with the baby, I think it's time for some tough love, kid."

"Meaning what?" I asked, inwardly cringing at what I knew would come next.

"It's time to face facts. You are not your mother."

"I know that," I shot back reflexively.

"Do you?" she challenged me. "Because last I checked, you were still emotionally closed off. You know, just because you love someone doesn't mean you have to be in constant fear of losing them or that, if you do, you will never be able to grieve and find a new normal again. What happened with your dad—"

"I get your point," I said. "But I don't agree with you. It might look that way, maybe, from the outside, but I don't think that's the problem. I just don't like being rushed."

"Fine, you want to prove you're not closed off? Let's take it to the *Lady's Journal*." She whipped her phone out of her pocket and thumbed the screen menacingly.

I raised my eyebrows. "What's a magazine going to tell us about whether I'm emotionally available? I mean, you're an amazing friend. You know that I'm there for you emotionally, right? I'm not a person who doesn't know how to love or something."

"For me, yes." Mandy nodded. "But with men, it's another story, and last month's personality quiz, 'Are You an Ice Princess?,' is going to prove it."

The Soul Mate 169

I tilted my head to the side. "Really? An ice princess?"

"Their words, not mine."

"Gee, thanks. I'm starting to think you only brought the donuts to soften the blow here." I dug in the brown bag and pulled out a glazed confection, then closed my eyes to focus on the sugary goodness in the hope of blocking out the carbohydrate carrying torture I'd just invited inside my private sanctuary.

"If I did, then it only goes to show how my master plan is working." She cleared her throat. "Okay, now, question one. When was the last time you told someone you loved them?" she asked.

"The last time I called my mother. So, a week ago," I said with not a little triumph.

She gave me the dead eyes and shook her head slowly. "Your mother obviously doesn't count."

"Where is that in the question?" I challenged her.

"It goes unspoken. Now, come on, get serious." Mandy shot back.

"Isn't this multiple choice?" I groaned.

"Not for you, it isn't. Stop stalling."

"What if I told you I love you right now?" I tried, desperate.

Mandy rolled her eyes. "A man, then. When was the last time you told a man you loved him?"

I bit down on my bottom lip. Before he died, I used to tell my father I loved him nearly every day. It had been one of the most important rules of growing up in my family. The world was a crazy place and anything could happen, so before it did, you made sure you told the people you loved that you loved them often and loudly. Before I left the house, whenever I called, whenever I went to bed, I told him. And then, when he'd gotten sick, those words had become a plea.

"I love you, Dad" became *"Please don't go"* or *"Don't leave us."*

And for my mother? She could hardly speak without bursting into tears during that time.

My own eyes burned as I shoved the memory away.

"Hello?" Mandy cleared her throat again. "You there?"

The Soul Mate 171

"Just thinking. I don't think this question counts for me. What if I have never been in love?"

Mandy pursed her lips. "Seems like a cop-out."

"Fine, fine. So, I told a boy in middle school that I loved him. I think that was the last time if you're not counting, you know, my dad or anything," I rushed through the second half of my sentence but it didn't matter—Mandy knew me too well to let it pass unnoticed.

"You haven't told a man you loved him since before your father died?" She raised her eyebrows.

"Maybe we should move on to the next question."

"Fine." Mandy glanced down at her phone, clicked something, then read, "How many dates does it take before you share personal details about your past?"

"I already told Mason about my past. He knows what my favorite childhood toy was and everything."

"Then he already knows about your mom and dad?" Mandy asked.

"Well, that's not fair. The specifics of it haven't really come up."

"Really? There was never an opening for you to tell him—the man who might be the father of your child—about your family? Not a single moment?"

I focused aggressively on my donut and licked at a bit of the glaze. "I don't think I like this pushy side of you."

"I'm your boss."

"Only at work," I reminded her. "And I don't think it's that important for Mason to know all my baggage so quickly. It's good to keep a little bit of mystery."

"Meaning you don't know any of his?"

I thought back to our night—the way he'd spoken about his mother's illness, the way some of his dreams had been snatched from him. "I know some of his history. I don't know that it counts as baggage."

"Right. So I'm guessing you want to skip this question too?" Mandy asked.

I took another bite of my donut, then washed it down with some latte. "I'm seriously not digging your tone."

The Soul Mate

Mandy shrugged. "You'll live. Now, come on, question three. How comfortable are you with sexual intimacy?"

"What kind of question is that?" I scoffed.

"A good one," Mandy said. "Now answer it."

"Well, I've already slept with him, so that sort of speaks for itself."

"It doesn't say how comfortable are you with sexuality. It says sexual intimacy," she pointed out.

"You know what? This quiz is stupid. You know me," I pleaded. "I'm not an ice princess."

"I see we've struck a nerve. Does this have anything to do with why you're still lying in bed?"

I took a sip of my coffee, opting not to answer.

Again, though, Mandy outsmarted me. "So you got intimate with him again and it was too much for you? Just say it."

"It wasn't that," I said, and the words poured from me like water breaking through a dam. "I told you. He wanted to give me a drawer at his place and after everything that's happened, it's just not something I'm ready for. I mean, I might have to get ready to be a mother. I don't think I can really handle falling in love on top of everything else. There's too much happening."

"So you think you're falling in love?" Mandy asked.

I set my coffee down, then leaned back against my pillows before huffing out a sigh. "That's not the point. The point is that I'm overwhelmed and he keeps pushing for more. I could have handled myself better but—"

"But you think you're falling for him?" Mandy asked again.

I leveled her with a stare. "I don't think. I know."

"And that scares you?"

"Scares me? It terrifies me." I shook my head. "But that's still not the important part. Mandy, what if I really am pregnant? I'll love my baby more than life itself. And if I love him, too – think about how much that is for someone like me to lose."

She closed her hand over mine and offered a gentle smile. "Then I'll remind you again. You're not your mother. And even if you were? Would it be so bad?"

I picked up my coffee, lost for words. "I'm done with this quiz."

Yup. Ice Princess it is. I may not admit it to Mandy but I have to admit it to myself. Now I have to figure out what to do with that knowledge.

"Fine," Mandy said. "But just…remember what we talked about, okay? The next time you see Mason?"

I nodded. "I will."

If there was a next time, at least. Because I was pretty sure if poor Devon thought I was a psycho, Mason had at least as much reason. If fact, I was starting to wonder if he'd ever want to talk to me again.

But what was even more worrisome was how awful that thought made me feel…

Broken and a little lost inside.

Chapter Eighteen

Mason

I swallowed hard, shifting the bag in my hands carefully before knocking on the door.

To be fair, I didn't know if she was home—she hadn't answered my text, and in light of my new discovery, I thought it was best not to send another. Instead, I opted to go straight to the source, readying to make things as right as I could.

If only Bren would let me.

A moment passed and I knocked again. I waited as I heard the muffled creak of floorboards and then, finally, met Bren's gaze as she opened the door. Her hair was covered by a fluffy white towel and she wore nothing but a silky robe that clung to her wet skin so that I could see the pert outlines of her nipples.

The look of her alone sent my mind reeling back to yesterday as she writhed in my arms.

Clearing my throat, I forced myself to focus, thrusting the bag in my hand toward her.

"Look, I think I messed up and I get it if you're not ready to talk, but I wanted you to know that I'm sorry. I was moving too fast and with everything else…I can see why it would have freaked you out."

She was quiet, her gaze locked on my outstretched hand, and she cocked her head.

"What's this?" she asked, then took the bag from me.

"It's candy."

"Did you rob a convenience store?" She rustled the bag, dipped in a hand and pulled out three different kinds of chocolate bars.

"I didn't know what you liked or if you were allergic to anything, so I just got everything and figured your favorite would be in there."

She fished through, taking her time, finally pulling out a package of Twizzlers. "You were right."

"Not a chocolate girl?"

She shook her head. "I mean, I like it, but not if there's licorice in the room. Uh"—she scrubbed a hand over the back of her neck as she stepped to the side—"did you want to come in?"

"I would love that." I entered her little foyer, then glanced around. The layout of her apartment was actually similar to my own, even if her little loft favored exposed brick to wide glass windows.

She closed the door behind me and led me to the khaki-colored sofa. Her lips tilted into a strained smile as she handed me the remote. "Turn on whatever you want. I'm going to put on some pants."

Part of me—the part I needed to keep a tight rein on—wanted to tell her not to. To ask her to stay here until she was ready for me to peel away that robe again. But instead I nodded and reached in my pocket, waiting until she had left the room to look at the envelope in my hands.

This, too, had been part of my plan. Maybe if the uncertainty of the baby was eliminated from the picture, we would be able to move forward like two rational adults. We would know how serious to be—how fast to move.

The Soul Mate 179

Maybe it had all been a dumb idea in the first place.

I ran over in my mind what I wanted to say, but then Bren reappeared and the words died in my throat. Even in gray yoga pants and a baggy T-shirt, she made my blood run hot, and I had to tear my gaze away. I couldn't even help the way my gaze traveled to her abdomen, struggling to see the tiniest hint of a bump.

"You didn't turn the TV on," she said.

"No," I said. "Look, I've been thinking and there are some things I want to tell you."

She crossed her arms over her tiny frame, her face wary again.

Shit.

Exactly the opposite of what I'd been going for here.

"Like what?" she asked.

"All we've got is this one life and mistakes are inevitable. We're going to fall short, we're going to fall flat on our ass sometimes, but the thing I don't want to do is be too afraid to say yes to something that makes me happy." I reached for the envelope again. "I guess what I'm really trying to say is that I know I messed up, but I don't want us to just walk away from each other like that and I think the real problem here is that we don't know how seriously to take any of this."

"So what do you think we should do?" she asked, her tone tentative.

"I think we should know, really know, whether you're pregnant or not."

For a long moment, she didn't say anything, and then she sighed and sank into a seat opposite me. "I've been thinking too. I flipped out when I shouldn't have. The whole...*intimacy* thing can get to me sometimes. And I have to admit, I don't like the uncertainty with regard to the baby question."

"Then let's take the uncertainty away. Let's open the envelope."

She looked from the envelope to me, then gave me one quick nod. "Yeah, you're probably right. We should know."

"Okay." I nodded.

"But maybe first, let's make it special or something."

She walked toward the mantel and snagged a large multicolored candle and a book of matches, then lit the match and made the candle glow. Taking the remote from me, she switched the channel to an indie folk station that hummed gently behind us.

"I should probably wear a dress in case we have to tell this story to our child one day, but I'm not going to change again," she said, running a self-conscious hand over her T-shirt.

"You look great just the way you are," I told her, and in the soft glow of the candle I could see her blush. "Okay," I said. "Let's find out."

I started to swipe my thumb under the flap, but she held out her hand, panic in her eyes.

"Over here, over near the candle. And…can you hold my hand?"

I ripped open the envelope, then moved toward her, closing my eyes as I took her hand. She squeezed so tight, I nearly let out a low whistle, marveling at her strength.

"Come on, already!" she whispered harshly.

With my free hand, I gripped the paper inside the envelope.

"Okay. We're—"

"Wait! Stop!" Bren practically screeched, and I turned to look at her, my heart thundering.

"Jesus, what? What's wrong?"

"I'm not ready. I don't want to know." She shook her head. "You were right. This whole time. You were right. We need to give this a chance regardless of the baby and without fear holding me back."

A slight smile tugged on my lips. "But the uncertainty. You said—"

"I know what I said, but first tell me, what are we? Are we together?"

I nodded. "That would be my choice."

She swallowed hard, not meeting my gaze as she spoke. "Mine too."

"So we are," I said simply. "We're together." I folded the envelope, tucked it back in my pocket, and then leaned down to cup Bren's chin. "I'll follow your lead with this baby and you let me know when you change your mind, okay?"

She nodded, and then I closed my lips over hers, savoring the rush of pure need that flooded my body whenever I touched her.

"You make me happy, Bren. Being with you makes me happy," I whispered. She rose on tiptoe to kiss me again, softer this time, and she stroked my jaw as she moved, brushing my stubble with her palm.

"You make me happy too," she whispered, and I kissed her again, weaving my fingers through her hair until she sighed against my mouth, letting my tongue slip between her lips to tease her.

Gently I stroked her tongue, coaxing another little moan from her as I wrapped my other hand around her waist and pulled her closer to me, until her body was flush with my own and she could feel the hard length of my need.

With every passing moment, every deep breath of her sweet, sweet perfume, that need grew stronger, until it threatened to gallop out of control. Even in the space of an instant, I found myself aching to be with her again, throbbing with the need to feel her tight and warm around me.

But first, I needed to show her exactly how happy she made me.

"Where's the bedroom?" I groaned.

She pulled away for a moment, her eyes hazy, and she pointed to the door on the far side of the room. "Do you have a condom?" she asked.

I nodded. I always kept one in my wallet for emergencies. "I have one. Just in case," I said, and then I took her hand and led her into the small, cluttered bedroom. Once inside, she wasted no time in stripping off her clothes, ripping her shirt over her head with so much force it sent her hair cascading down her back.

"Slowly," I said, taking another step toward her and gripping her waist. "Unless you want me to do it for you?"

I trailed my fingers along the smooth outline of her spine, then found the clasp of her bra.

I might have been exposed to the female form every day in my line of work, but that didn't make my moments with Bren any less special. I knew it took a lot for her to share her body with me.

With a quick flick of the wrist, I released her from the confines of her bra and moved to rub the sensitive swell of her breasts and stroke the pretty tips of her nipples.

"Beautiful," I murmured, and she grinned at me.

"You're not being fair. You still have your clothes on."

"Then let me level the playing field." Releasing her nipple, I gripped the hem of my shirt and dragged it over my head, letting it fall onto the floor with her clothes. Then, slowly, I reached for my jeans, unbuttoning and unzipping them in short order before dragging them down to my ankles along with my boxers.

As I stepped from my clothes, I heard her let out a little gasp, and I grinned. "You all right?"

She shook her head. "I don't know how I keep forgetting."

"What's that?" I reached for her pants, undoing them like I had my own, trying not to drown in the scent of her and the weight of my own need.

"How...*big* you are."

I grinned. "We both know how well you handle it, gorgeous. It's going to be so good."

She wet her lips and then hooked her thumbs under the slender strip of lace that held up her panties, ready to drag them off and show me the narrow trail of down that led to the place I longed to see most.

But then, just as she was about to step from her clothes, she started to sink to her knees in front of me.

"No," I said, my voice more coarse than I'd expected. I couldn't let her do that—not because I didn't want her to. I wanted to feel her mouth around me more than almost anything in the world. But today wasn't about me. It was all for Bren.

"Get on the bed," I commanded. "And spread your legs for me. I want to look at you."

She gazed up at me, her eyes wide, and for a moment I thought she might argue, but then she straightened and pushed aside her tangled sheets, making room for herself on the mattress.

When she lay there, her knees spread apart so I could see her sweet pink center, I stared for a long moment, my mouth watering, and shook my head. "Damn, you're so fucking perfect," I muttered as a pretty pink blush overtook her cheeks.

"I want you. I want to feel you inside me," she whispered, parting her knees to lure me even closer.

I fought the desire to give in, to slide forward and take her hard and fast, as I shook my head again. "Not yet."

Making my way to the edge of the bed, I commanded her to scoot toward me, and then I sank onto my knees until my mouth was level with her body. Slowly, gently, I kissed the insides of her knees, licking my way along the silky skin of her inner thighs until she shivered and writhed at my touch. My cock swelled as goose bumps lit up her flesh, a visual cue that she wanted me as badly as I wanted her right now.

"Mason," she called, tugging at my wrist. "Please," she panted, "I need you."

And that might have been true. But I wasn't giving in—not yet. I knew about the female anatomy. I knew that less was more, and women required gentler touches than men. And I wanted her nice and wet when I finally sank inside her.

When I was done with my teasing, I stroked her swollen core with my thumb, focusing on the rise and fall of her breasts as she took short, frantic breaths. She was so slick, so welcoming, it was like torture to deny her.

"You're trying to kill me," she said.

I blew out a harsh laugh and prayed for patience. "You have no idea. This is as hard on me as it is on you."

She leaned up to meet my gaze, but the heat behind her eyes told me everything I needed to know. Massaging her thighs again, I leaned down and licked her soft pink folds, dragging my tongue along her slit until I found the tight bundle of nerves I was seeking.

Slowly I circled her center. She dropped back into the mattress, pulsing against my mouth almost involuntarily as I sucked and licked and rolled my tongue in time with every little quake of her body.

"Mason, please," she cried, arching toward me, driving her fingers into my hair. "Please."

But it was all too good. Pushing one finger inside her waiting channel, I pistoned inside her, feeling her tighten and quake as she ground into my finger, my mouth, working herself against me to slake her need.

"I'm going to come," she moaned. "I want you to feel me. Please, please, I want you to."

It was an offer I couldn't refuse.

Something inside me snapped and, still teasing her with my tongue, I fumbled for the condom on the floor and quickly rolled it over my aching, throbbing shaft.

"Yes," she breathed. "Hurry, please."

So I did. Grasping her hips, I rose to my feet and pulled her onto my length, plunging myself hard and deep until I was buried to the hilt. There was no denying what she'd said was true—she was close. Right on the edge. So tight, and so perfect. I could feel her walls fluttering all around me already. I closed my eyes and let out a deep breath before I began my steady, rhythmic thrusts. Moving slower than I wanted to, but wanting her to feel every firm inch of me.

"You feel so good," she moaned, and I stared down at her, knowing that I could never explain in words exactly how good *she* felt. It was like the end of a thousand days of winter to be inside her again. She set me on fire.

"Touch yourself for me, baby," I commanded hoarsely, and as her hand dropped between her thighs, I watched her fingers toy with the space my tongue had been only moments ago.

"Yeah, that's it," I praised her. "Now tell me how good it feels."

"It feels amazing. It feels like…" She shook her head, but I knew what she meant. There were no words. She let out a low moan.

Her walls tightened around me, and though I wanted to spend all night inside her, the call of her body was simply too strong. Watching her breasts bounce as I moved, her hand working her sensitive bud, I was hovering closer and closer to the edge. As my balls drew up, I knew there was no choice left.

Gripping her hips harder, I moved inside her with everything I had, thrusting in and out with quick, needy bursts. She gasped, gripping the sheet beneath her as she moaned my name.

"Mason, Mason, I'm going to come," she said.

"Then come for me, baby," I growled.

She wasted no time. Her walls squeezed me so

tight I saw stars and I held her hips tighter, afraid that I would be swept away by the sheer power of her orgasm. But before I could focus on her for too long, I broke apart myself. Euphoria spread through my body, making me lose all sense of self.

My mouth dropped open and I pushed into her as I came with her, working her body for every last drop of pleasure before finally releasing her and collapsing onto the bed beside her.

Chapter Nineteen

Bren

"That big bag of candy is sounding awfully good right about now."

Mason chuckled at me from the bed.

I pulled on my pants, then turned around to look at Mason, still lying against my pillow and staring at me with those penetrating blue eyes of his. I was still scared shitless, but with every touch and every minute we spent together, I was starting to wonder if maybe it really could be this good with someone. This easy…

"Hungry?" he asked, but in response his own stomach rumbled.

I laughed.

"I guess it is about time for it," he said, glancing at the digital clock on my nightstand. He moved to sit on the edge of the bed and swung his feet to the floor.

"No, don't get up." I yanked my shirt over my head and then rushed toward him. "Stay naked and we can order a pizza and eat in bed."

Something about leaving this space and the cocoon of my room made me feel angsty. Like it might break the spell or pop the little bubble of happiness I was living in.

"I can get naked again whenever you need me to," he said. "But if you're not staying naked while we wait for the delivery guy, then I'm not either." The mattress springs creaked as he got up and grabbed his pants. As he shoved his legs into his jeans, he glanced down at the floor, and I followed his gaze to find that the ripped white envelope had fallen out of his pocket.

"Yeah," I said, swallowing past the growing tension in the room. Damn. For that hour there, I'd nearly forgotten all about that little white piece of paper.

Liar.

"You're right," I said, suddenly feeling like I was in a prison cell instead of a cocoon. "It might be good to get some food outside the house. There's a pizza place around the corner open if you don't mind my wearing this."

He shook his head. "Not at all."

Inwardly, I let out a little sigh as he pulled his shirt back on, hiding his contoured abs from view.

"All right, I'll grab my purse." Finding it in its usual spot, I took my clutch and led the way from the apartment building down to the row of little shops around the corner.

"There's a river not far from here. It's beautiful in the spring. One of the only places in the city where you can still fish."

"You fish?" He raised his eyebrows and I nodded.

I opened my mouth and closed it. Then, thinking of what Mandy had said, I started again. "My, um, my dad and I used to go on fishing trips when I was little. He's the one who taught me."

"That sounds like a nice memory. Do you still go?"

My throat went dry. "No."

That seemed like enough sharing for now. For a second I wanted to pat myself on the back, but I knew, even in my own warped mind, that wasn't nearly enough.

We walked into the building and, lucky for me, Mason's attention was captured by the glowing neon sign listing the restaurant's specials. In a matter of seconds, a waitress appeared and led us to a table with windows that overlooked the river I'd been talking about.

"Seems like we're destined to eat on the water," I said. "First the golf course, now here."

Mason nodded. "I like it. It's…romantic."

Less romantic was the pile of appetizers we got—a mountain of fried goodness that was destined to make us feel awful for days to come. Still, I couldn't help but inwardly squeal at the thought of lots and lots of garlic knots dipped in spicy marinara.

Was that a pregnancy craving, or just a garden-variety craving? My thoughts tripped back to the white envelope and my throat went tight.

"So." He eyed me warily, and I cut in.

"What is it? What's the matter?" I asked, almost paranoid that he could read my thoughts.

He shook his head. "Nothing, nothing. I just… I kind of want to talk about the baby. If you don't mind."

"I don't mind." I shrugged, sort of relieved I wasn't alone in this. "I think about her a lot."

"Her?" he asked, cocking a brow my way.

I slapped my hand over my mouth. "Oh my gosh," I murmured. "I didn't even realize. I mean, I've sort of been calling her a girl in my head."

"Does it feel like a girl?" he asked softly. "Have you been having symptoms?"

A rush of heat flooded to my cheeks. "I wasn't going to tell you, but I have been having some, definitely not a lot, but a *few* symptoms."

"Like what?" he asked, sipping on his soda.

"Well." I cleared my throat. "My, uh, breasts? They've been really tender. And I also, maybe, have an increased libido. Possibly," I added, my cheeks flaming.

His mouth spread into a wolf's grin, and for a moment I wondered whether he was proud of himself for amping up my sex drive or if the idea that this baby might be real was too much for him to hold inside. Whatever the case, though, I found myself beaming back.

I grabbed a mozzarella stick and a knot of buttery bread.

"Have you had any cravings?" he asked.

"Well, I'm dying for these garlic knots," I said. "I don't know what counts as a craving, though. My mother ate lemons whole when she was pregnant with me."

"Are you serious?" he asked with a chuckle. "I've heard some women tell me whacky things, but I don't recall hearing that one before."

I nodded. "Dead serious. My dad brought home limes because the store was out of lemons once and she chucked them at his head until he went to another store and found some."

"That's intense," Mason said. "So are you telling me I should get a helmet just in case?" he teased.

"Couldn't hurt," I said with a laugh. "But, yeah, if that's the response to a craving, then, no. I don't feel the urge to pelt you with food."

"Are you sure? Because I'll duck."

"Don't you dare. If I'm carrying your baby, you'd better let me hit you with all the garlic knots I want."

His smile warmed and sent a thrill through me. "Okay, fine. Deal."

"Deal." I nodded, then picked up a garlic knot and tossed it at him.

He snagged it out of thin air without even blinking and I gasped.

"I can read you like a book," he said before taking a triumphant bite.

That may be true and I'm not sure how I feel about it.

"I guess I just have to use the element of surprise next time." I shrugged and then took a bite of my own food.

When Mason finished chewing, he said, "So, you think about her a lot?"

"I do." I nodded.

"What do you think about?"

"Oh, I don't know. I guess I sort of think about what her nursery would look like and what kinds of things we could do together as she gets older. Teaching her to walk."

"And fish," Mason added, and my heart broke a little bit.

I *had* thought about that. Often. And I still hadn't decided if it would break my heart to do it without my dad there or help me heal some.

"Yes, and fish," I said quietly.

"Do you think you're going to be an overly protective mom?"

"Why? You planning on taking her skydiving?"

"Not until she's at least fifteen."

"Eighteen," I countered.

"Eighteen, then. No, I was thinking of teaching her to work on cars and how to ride horses."

"You ride horses?" I asked.

He nodded. "I have cousins in Montana who own a ranch. I used to go there every summer to help out. My parents thought it was important that I get a full sense of the world."

"Well, anything with animals is okay in my book," I said. "Just don't let her treat your patients or anything until after medical school."

"We've decided on medical school for her already?" he asked with a laugh.

"It's the family business," I shrugged. "It seems likely, don't you think? Plus, on her first Halloween we can get her tiny scrubs and a little stethoscope. How cute would that be?"

"You really have been thinking about this a lot, huh?" he asked softly.

I nodded. "A lot. And I want what's best for us. Which is why…when we're done here, I think we ought to go back to my place and find out what's inside that envelope. I'm being a chickenshit and it's time to rip this Band-Aid off once and for all."

He nodded encouragingly. "I think that's the right thing to do."

I realized for the first time that he always wanted to open the envelope. He'd only been waiting for me. And the anticipation must have been killing him. I think in that moment I fell a little in love and instead of fighting it, I pulled the feeling closer and let it wrap around me like a warm blanket.

We waited for the check, which he paid like a gentleman, and then we walked back onto the street with our hands laced together.

"I like the idea of a tiny you," he said.

"A tiny me?" I asked.

"Yeah." He swung our hands back and forth between us. "Maybe she'll be a veterinarian. A little bit of you and a little bit of me."

"Makes sense." I sighed. "Whatever she becomes, we know she'll be smart."

"If she has half your brains, she'll be just fine."

"I would say the same about you." We stopped in front of my complex, and he leaned down and kissed me just as a raindrop fell on my shoulder. Slowly I wrapped my arms around his neck and fell into his kiss, pushing and pulling along with his tongue until my head swam.

I didn't know if I was stalling or simply taken by the moment, but whatever it was, when he pulled away, the last thing I wanted to do was follow him inside.

Instead I wanted to stay out here in the rain, in his arms, breathing in the uncertainty of a family that I only just now realized how badly I wanted.

It had been so long since I'd had a family that was whole and happy and good. To have this baby…to have the chance to mend the broken pieces of my heart that my father's death had left behind…it would be such a blessing. But I had to take that terrifying first step.

Mason took my hand and led me into the building, stopping only when we reached my front door.

I pulled out my keys and unlocked it, then led him inside, ignoring the sudden tightness in my chest.

"Time for round two," I said, then found the matches and lit every candle in the room until the whole place was filled with glowing yellow light. Mason ducked into my bedroom, and when he reappeared, he held the white envelope—and our fate—in his hands.

I took a deep breath then turned on the indie folk station again, closing my eyes as the music filled my head and dulled the insistent pounding of my heart.

"We don't have to do this." His deep voice rumbled through the room, and I opened my eyes again to find Mason waiting for me.

"No," I said, taking another step toward him and the tall pillar candle in the center of my coffee table. Thought nerves swam in my belly, I knew it was time. "I want to know. Once and for all."

He nodded. "Then let's find out."

He handed me the envelope and I blinked back at him. "But I thought—"

"You've been patient with me and you agreed to my crazy scheme. You should be the one to open the envelope."

I swallowed hard, then nodded. "Okay, fine, but come close so we see it at the same time."

He took another step toward me, wrapping one of his arms around my shoulders as I held the envelope in my now trembling hands.

This was it. The moment of truth.

"Whatever this paper says…" I started, but I had no words. Shaking my head, I wet my lips, then said, "Maybe we ought to count down?"

"That's a great idea. On three?" he asked.

"On three," I agreed.

"One," he said.

"Two," I sighed.

"Three." We said the last word in unison, and I tore the final scrap of paper from inside the envelope and stared down at it as Mason's arm squeezed me close to his hot, hard chest.

But the words weren't right and they blurred before me. They weren't the ones I'd been expecting. And when I closed my eyes at night?

The words weren't the ones I'd seen in my dreams.

Mason's arm loosened from my shoulders and he stepped back before I turned to face him.

"Not pregnant," I said through numb lips, though the words alone made me suddenly want to burst into tears. "Are you relieved?"

I could hear myself talking and it sounded echoey to my own ears as I tried to quell the sudden wash of nausea that swept over me.

"No," he said simply, his blue gaze searching mine. "Not at all."

"Me, neither," I admitted, swiping a trembling hand over my eyes. "Shit. How accurate is this?"

"It's accurate, Bren."

Confusion, fear and disappointment washed over me. "I think I need a drink."

I blew out the candle on the coffee table and stalked toward the little bar cart in the entryway. Carefully I selected the best bottle of whiskey I had—though in truth it was also the only bottle—and poured two glasses.

Making my way back to him, I held out a glass and he took it without a word.

"I thought…" I started, but everything I'd thought sounded dumb now. Unimportant.

I took a sip of my drink and winced at the burning oaky flavor that hit me even harder considering I hadn't had a drink in so long. I couldn't. Not when I'd thought I was having a baby.

A million questions rushed through my head, but I didn't have the nerve to ask a single one of them. Instead, I settled onto my couch and stared down at my glass, wondering about what this would mean for me. What it would mean for us. He had no reason to stay here now, to make this budding relationship work. And I had no reason to ask him to.

Only a couple of hours or so ago, we'd daydreamed together about a baby girl who was smart and brave and wonderful, pledged that we were together, but that had been when there was a potential baby in the mix. Now that we knew there wasn't? There was no telling how Mason's feelings might have changed. Maybe this was the end of the road.

But it was more than that. I felt like, even though there had never been a baby, the child between us had gone. Like all my hopes and dreams for the baby I'd wanted so much were dashed in that one terrible moment.

And just like a tragedy, the death of hope left grief in its wake.

"So," Mason said, and then took a sip of his own drink.

I followed suit, then said, "So."

We stared at one another, suddenly aware of a stark, tense awkwardness that had never been more present…not even the day my feet had been in stirrups. Which, I supposed, made sense, because suddenly there was simply nothing left to say. We had nothing to do, nothing to plan. The vitamins he'd given me were useless. All of our past conversations on the topic were just silly dreams.

It was all gone, replaced instead with crushing, all-consuming disappointment.

"I have to get up early," I said. "I wonder if—"

"Yeah, sure. I'd better get going anyway. I've got a big day ahead of me as well," he said, and though we both knew we were just making lame excuses, I nodded. Clearly we both needed some time to process this and didn't need an audience while we did it. It was a lot to take in.

I followed him to the door, taking his half-full glass before waving him off and embracing the sudden stillness of the apartment.

"Night," he said stiffly.

"Night," I returned before closing the apartment door.

There were no sweet embraces, no tender goodnight kisses, no promises to call tomorrow.

As I took a deep breath and stalked toward the bar cart for a refill, I realized there were things to be grateful for. Loads of them. Now I wouldn't have to move or know the financial burden of a child. I wouldn't go through morning sickness or cravings. I wouldn't have stretch marks or pee when I coughed too hard. I wouldn't gain weight. Hallelujah, am I right?

I wouldn't have a baby.

With shaky hands, I brought the whiskey to my lips and took a long sip.

I glanced at the door behind me, then leaned back until my back hit the wood of the door. I slid all the way to the ground, crumpling until my head rested on my knees and I saw the world from an angle as big and overwhelming as it felt.

I wouldn't have a baby.

I couldn't understand it any more than I could understand why the weight of loss was pressing so hard and deep on my chest. Leaning my head back against the wood of the door, I tried again to take a deep breath, but instead I gasped out a sob as a scalding tear rolled down my cheek and dripped onto my shirt.

First one, then another and another until I was crying, mourning the loss of something that had never been mine to begin with.

I wasn't having Mason's baby.

Chapter Twenty
Mason

I felt like I'd been holding my breath ever since I'd left Bren's apartment last night.

As Mondays went, it was even worse than usual—complete with a drab, rainy sky and the promise of a stilted lunch with only one of my parents instead of both of them. Because, from now on, that was how I'd be seeing them most of the time now—separately.

After my second appointment of the day, I trudged back to my office, determined to get some work done if only to feel slightly accomplished on top of whatever else this deluge of disappointment and confusion had already caused.

As soon as I sat down, though, Trent walked in behind me, knocking on the open door before stepping in front of my desk.

"Why aren't you ready to go?"

I closed my eyes, then opened them again, trying

to hide my exasperation and all-around exhaustion. I'd barely slept when I got home last night. Instead, I'd spent the whole of the evening pacing, thinking about Bren, wondering if I ought to have stayed longer to comfort her. As potential motherhood had been ripped away from her, I'd behaved like an asshat when I could have and should have been her rock. If she didn't trust me anymore, I wouldn't blame her. But the again…maybe she'd never really trusted me at all.

Not that I had any way of knowing how she felt to begin with. She hadn't answered the text I'd sent last night when I'd gotten home, and she'd seemed to need some space. I'd already made the mistake of crowding her once and I wasn't about to do it again.

"Dude, what is up with you?" Trent asked.

"I'm sorry, man. Distracted is all. Where am I supposed to be going?"

Trent's mouth became a thin line as he tilted his head to the side. "It's our day in neonatal. We've got to be there in ten minutes and we obviously also have to stop for a decent-sized coffee for you on the way."

"I'm fine," I shot back.

"You have purple bags under your eyes. Now, come on. Grab your coat. Coffee's on me."

I did as he asked, then followed him down the hall, stopping only to instruct my assistant which calls to take and which to get messages for. Paramount, obviously, was to call me if Bren phoned the office. Though of course, now that she wasn't pregnant, she'd have no reason to.

"You know what? Just get messages from everyone," I corrected myself, then followed Trent through the open door and into the wide, drearily lit atrium.

Rain flecked the wide skylights, and I glanced up briefly before turning back to Trent.

"Okay, I could probably do with a coffee," I admitted.

"No kidding," Trent said, still leading me through the revolving door and onto the street. Our private practice wasn't far from the hospital—convenient for when our patients went into labor—and luckily there was a Starbucks just next door to both.

I walked into the dim little cafe and got into the

The Soul Mate 213

line, only vaguely aware that Trent still stood beside me as I waited. After I'd ordered, though, we stood at the delivery counter, and from my peripheral vision I could see him surveying me warily.

"What's wrong?" I asked.

"I should ask you the same thing. You've been a zombie all day and you love going to neonatal but you aren't even smiling."

"I'm just not in a baby mood today," I said.

Trent squinted at me as my name was called and I collected my coffee.

"You're in a rough field to not be in a baby mood," Trent said with a short laugh.

"I know, I know. Look, things have just been weird for me lately. Besides, what's with the third degree? Why don't we talk about you for a change?"

"Because I actually have my shit together. You, on the other hand—"

"Hey," I said. "Look, I've got a lunch date with my mom later and I'm just weirded out about how it's going to be now that my parents are splitting up. I think people always mean for these things to go amicably and then it turns into a bloodbath, so."

Trent shook his head. "Nope. I don't think that's it."

"I'm telling you it is, though."

"Look, I get that the whole parental thing is weird."

"It's beyond weird. I've only known them together my whole life and now it's going to be an adjustment. I'll get over it."

Trent nodded. "My parents have been divorced for a long time. It's going to be strange at first and it's going to be worse when they start dating again, but it'll work out. I've known your dad for a long time. He's not the sort of guy who lets things get ugly if he can help it, and your mom seems great."

"I know. That's true." I took a deep breath. "And I guess that's not all of it either."

"No?" Trent said. "Color me shocked."

"Just humor me here, okay?" I said. "So Bren and I opened the envelope last night."

The Soul Mate 215

"I figured," Trent said, nodding.

"What, are you a mind reader now, too?"

"No, Bren called and canceled a checkup we had on the books," Trent said.

"At least I know her phone is still working. I have no evidence of that myself."

Trent shrugged. "People handle things in different ways. But hey, you both dodged a bullet, right?"

"Right," I sighed. "I just wish it felt that way."

"It doesn't?"

"No. I mean, you'd think I'd be thrilled not to have a baby with a virtual stranger, but over these last two weeks we've just gotten closer, you know? Like, even in such a short period, I feel really connected to her."

Trent led me through the hospital's revolving doors but didn't say anything.

"What?" I prompted.

"I don't know, man. This is some deep shit."

I nodded. "I know. It's insane. It makes no sense to be disappointed."

"And how does she feel?" Trent asked.

"I don't know. I left almost right after we found out and she hasn't answered my texts since. She seemed as upset as I was, though. It seemed like I'd just gotten her to open up a little and the news sealed her right back up, tighter than before."

"Maybe she is upset," Trent said. "Did she want children? Neither one of you are getting any younger. Biological clock and all that shit."

"She wanted the baby, I think. She didn't say it in as many words, but I think we both wanted the baby."

"Well, the baby isn't happening so, from my perspective, you need to figure something else out."

"Like what?"

"Like whether, now that you're not going to be a family, you still want to see this girl and maybe have a family with her down the line."

"I do. Absolutely. But if she won't answer my text—"

"Then you need to figure out how to get back on the right track. The Mason I know doesn't give up at the first sign of a challenge."

We walked into the neonatal unit and a nurse approached us, briefing us on which babies needed to be rocked or fed. I picked up the first little girl she'd pointed to—a tiny thing with delicate pink skin and a shock of dark hair.

Taking a bottle from the nurse, I fed the little girl, rocked her in my arms, and held back another rush of regret as I stared into her wide blue eyes. She was perfect in every way. Beautiful. Just like I'd pictured my own daughter for that brief, shining moment yesterday evening.

"You okay?" Trent asked as he rocked a baby boy.

I nodded. "Yup. Just realizing that for once, you're right, man. I need to figure out something and quick. If I don't, I'm going to be letting the woman I want get away."

Now the only question was what exactly I needed to do to get her to realize that there was more than just this baby that never was between us.

"Now you're thinking. Shit, maybe you should

take her away for the weekend, make a grand gesture and all that," Trent said. "Women love that shit."

He was right. We needed the focus back on me and Bren. Start fresh. Someplace that was totally different from all the places we'd been when we were thinking we might become a family. A chance to start over.

I glanced down at the baby in my arms, then settled her back in her crib before I pulled my phone from my lab coat pocket.

"Trent, any chance you can cover for me today?" I asked.

Trent frowned. "Yeah, all right. Everything okay?"

I nodded. "Totally fine. I'm going to do it."

"Do what?"

"Take Bren away."

Trent chuckled. "I didn't mean today, dude."

"No time like the present."

If she wasn't answering my message, I had to send one she had no choice but to respond to.

With quick fingers, I typed, *"Get ready. We're leaving in an hour."*

Then, when I heard the chime letting me know the message had been sent, I called the zoo and asked to be transferred to the head of endangered animals. Then I waited until a clear, chirpy female voice filled the line.

"Mandy with the City Zoo. How can I help you today?"

"Hi, Mandy. This is Mason. I'm calling in reference to Bren Matthew's schedule."

There was a slight pause, and then she said, "What about it?"

"Well, I have a few questions. First, is she there today?"

"Not until this afternoon," she replied slowly. "It's her late night. Why?"

"Would it be possible to rearrange the schedule so that Bren didn't come in to work for a few days? It's important."

Another pause. "Is this Dr. Bentley?"

"It is."

Her next long pause made my gut tense, but then she spoke.

"I think I can manage that, Mason," Mandy said. "I'm guessing it's for a surprise?"

"It is."

"Well, have fun and don't let my girl tell you no. She can be stubborn."

Relief shot through me at her words, but I was only halfway to the goal line. I still had no idea if my Hail Mary for a touchdown was going to backfire or win Bren over.

"I won't." I hung up the phone, then glanced at Trent. "I can reschedule my next couple days of appointments, but other than that, you're sure you can handle things here?"

He nodded. "I'll hold down the fort. Just text me your itinerary when you have one so I know when you'll be back."

The phone in my pocket chimed and I dug it out to find a response from Bren.

"Can't. Work tonight."

I typed back a rapid reply:

"Not anymore. Bring clothes for warm weather."

I could tell she read my response and when she didn't reply for five minutes, I launched into action. Might as well take that as a yes.

The next hour was a rush of buying luggage and tickets, along with reserving a last-minute villa, but when I finally arrived at Bren's door an hour later, it was with a deep sense of satisfaction. This was going to work. I had no doubt about that. I just had to get Bren to see it, too.

I knocked on the door and it flew open without warning. Bren stood facing me, her arms crossing over her slender frame, and I smiled as I took in her pretty purple sundress.

"Ready to go?" I asked.

"You called my boss?" she asked, her gaze wary.

"Yes, but it was important. And I have a gift for you to make up for it." I grabbed the tiny pink bag with matching pink tissue paper and held it out for her to take. For a moment, she eyed it with suspicion, then took it and dug past the tissue paper to pull out a navy bikini with a jeweled design near each of the hips.

"A bikini?" she said.

"For our trip. Now tell me you pulled out clothes. I got you a suitcase, too."

I walked past her into the house, then stalked into her bedroom to find a small pile of clothing on the bed.

"Laundry or luggage?" I asked.

"Uh, luggage. But I'm not sure—"

"We need to get away from everything for a little while. I'll admit that my idea was dumb, but we need to recalculate and start fresh. I got a private villa in the Cayman Islands for the next few days and everything has been arranged. Our plane is waiting and everything is set. All you need to do is say yes, Bren. Say yes to taking a chance. With me."

She blinked at me, the bikini dangling from her hand. And then her wide, round eyes were even rounder. "You planned all this? Even though we're not…"

She didn't have to say the last word and let it fall unspoken between us. We both knew what it was.

"I planned everything because I meant what I

said. You make me happy. Baby or no baby. And if you ask me, it's the perfect time to grab our bathing suits and get out of this miserable weather."

The rain tapped against her windows as I spoke, and she glanced to look at the storm outside before nodding and turning shining eyes toward me. "Okay. Yes. Yes, I'll go away with you."

Together we packed her things then made our way to the airport.

It was a rush to make it through security and to our gate, but once we were safely on the plane and in the air, Bren turned to me, her cheeks pink.

"So, what do you have planned for when we get there?"

"I think we need to get back to basics. Do things right this time."

"You mean you're going to meet me all over again?" she asked.

I shrugged. "Maybe. You want to pretend we're two strangers who happened to book the same house overnight and we've got only one bed to share?"

"I like the idea of only having one bed." Her eyes danced with excitement and a rush of need shot through me.

Fuck me, this might actually work.

I made a mental note to send Trent a beer-of-the-month-club membership.

"Me, too," I said, then brushed her cheek with my hand as I leaned in for a slow, soft kiss. "Nice to meet you, Ashley Brennan Matthews."

"Nice to meet you, Mason…some middle name Bentley," she said.

I laughed. "Andrew."

"Mason Andrew. I like it." She gave me an approving nod.

"There's something I want to tell you," she said, voice going softer.

"You can tell me anything, you know that."

She nodded, and took a deep breath, steeling herself for whatever was on her mind. "I should have told you a long time ago. We lost my dad when I was sixteen…"

I reached out and took her hand, rubbing gentle circles on the back of her knuckles. I hadn't expected her to choose this moment to finally open up, but I was grateful she was letting me in.

"I'm so sorry. Cancer?"

She nodded. I felt like a fool about all those times I'd told her about my mom—my mom had won her battle while Bren's dad hadn't. I imagined how hard that must have been for her to sit and listen to my stories. No wonder she'd chosen to remain silent and stoic.

I held her hand through the entire conversation, listening attentively and even wiping away the stray tear that escaped and tumbled down her cheek at one point. When it was done, she seemed so relieved, like maybe I could shoulder some of the burden that had been weighing her down for so many years. We didn't talk for a long time after that, I just continued holding her hand, and stroking her fingers with mine.

Then she leaned her head on my shoulder and we put on our headphones, both of us settling in to watch the in-flight movie before falling asleep.

When we arrived, it took a solid hour to get to

our villa, since it was secluded from the other, more tourist-friendly hotels. It was a little house that sat on the white sandy shore, with an outdoor hot tub, pool, and shower inviting us to enjoy the gorgeous sunset.

Me and Bren, alone.

Like in my apartment, there were wide glass windows that looked out on the rolling ocean, and when I led her into the little loft-style room inside, she sucked in a breath.

"What?" I asked.

She shook her head. "It's just so beautiful. I couldn't have imagined anything like this. I mean, one minute I was just getting ready for work and the next I'm here. Tell me, do you plan to make a habit of this?"

"What?"

Her eyes softened. "Turning my whole world upside down in the best possible way."

"If you'll let me," I said, the last of the ice that had been building in my chest since the night before melting.

"Good." She nodded. "I want you to."

As Bren unpacked, I made us some drinks from the items I'd ordered ahead, then pulled the fresh fish from the fridge and started the grill.

"You might not have needed the bikini," I said. "This place is pretty secluded."

"I'll keep that in mind," she said as she stepped into the kitchen in her tiny navy swimsuit. She took her drink from my outstretched hand, then said, "Let's wait on the fish. Let's just go watch the sunset, okay?"

"Okay." I nodded, then followed her out onto the deck, taking a seat beside her on the swinging bench.

"This was romantic of you, you know that?"

"I'm glad you like it," I told her, and as I looked at her in the fading evening light, I felt like she still deserved more. Everything I could give her would never be enough. Baby or no, the warm swell I felt in my chest when I looked at Bren made me understand one thing—I was going to do my damnedest to make this work.

Come hell or high water.

Chapter Twenty-One

Bren

"What an amazing day." I let out a groan and dropped onto the bed, my muscles sore and legs trembling.

"You killed it on that hike. I was impressed." Mason sat down on the mattress beside me, smiling down at me.

We'd just spent the day hiking in the beautiful Crystal Caves, and then followed it up with paddle-boarding in the Caribbean.

It had been exhilarating, and I'd been amazed to see how well our personalities meshed. From the moment we'd arrived in paradise, Mason and I had been on the same page with every decision. Skip breakfast and grab coffee to go or sit down for a leisurely brunch? Nap or go for a walk on the beach? It was nice to see how well we got along, how easy he was to be with.

I also got to see how he handled challenges. Like when we got to the rental car counter and found that they'd messed up his reservation, and didn't have any available cars for the next three hours. For a moment there, my heart had sunk. He'd tried to pull together the perfect weekend and we'd only just landed when already something was going wrong. I took a deep breath, turning to watch how Mason would react. But rather than blowing his cool, he rolled with it. He arranged for us to get a ride to our rental house and negotiated for an upgraded car to be dropped off to us later. The memory made me smile.

"What's next on the agenda?" I asked, almost afraid to hear what he might say. All this touring paradise and I was exhausted.

"Hmm." Mason reached out, rubbing my shoulders. "You look a little flushed from all that activity today. Do you want a nap?"

I shook my head. I wasn't sleepy. "Maybe just something low-key."

"I'm thinking we go cool off in the pool with a frozen drink. You in?"

My mouth lifted in a smile. "It's like you can read my mind."

He leaned down and pressed a soft kiss to my mouth. "You're perfect."

He'd told me that so many times, I was starting to believe him. Wrapping my hands around his neck, I pulled him in for another kiss. "Thank you for all of this."

He met my gaze, and his eyes softened. "It's not just me—you're feeling this, right?"

"*This?*" I challenged, smirking at him. Wasn't it the common joke that men couldn't talk about their feelings? For Mason and me, that was reversed. He was so open and loving, and I was the guarded one.

He took my hand and pressed it over his heart. "Yes. This. Everything that's developing between us."

The steady thump of his heart under my palm sped up. I nodded. "It's been fast, but yes, I'm very much feeling this."

In that moment, I sensed that he wanted to say more, maybe even the L-word. His eyes already revealed what his lips held back. But the only thing that scared me was how badly I wanted to say it back to him.

With one last kiss pressed to my forehead, Mason rose to his feet. "Go get changed into your swimsuit and I'll make a batch of piña coladas."

"You're perfect," I murmured.

"Careful now, Bren. Don't you go falling in love with me." He shot a wide grin over his shoulder.

"Why, Dr. Bentley. Would that be a problem for you?" Part of me couldn't believe the boldness of my words, but the other part of me? The one that wanted to be rash and brazen and emotional? She had already fallen for him. That day when he delivered prenatal vitamins to me. Even more so when he stuck by me even after finding out I wasn't pregnant. Most guys would have cut and run, relieved at the idea of not being tied down with a kid. But not Mason.

His expression turned more serious, his eyes blazing on mine. "Not for me. Just be ready to give me forever."

Then his tight ass was retreating toward the kitchen, and I lay there, my heart pounding.

We might not have been brave enough to say those three little words yet, but I knew in my heart what I felt—overwhelming love—like I never thought I'd experience.

The man was gifted in the bedroom, he cooked, and was even-tempered, sweet, romantic, and passionate about his work delivering babies. Plus he got my love for animals. Not only that, he accepted my crazy fear of commitment, giving me the space I needed to close the gap between us all on my own.

I was falling hard and fast, and I didn't want to stop.

Heaving myself up off the bed moments later, I snatched my swimsuit from the open suitcase at the foot of the bed and headed for the bathroom.

When I got into the bathroom to change, my smile fell. Just perfect. I'd started my period. Of all the days for this to happen? On vacation...really, universe? I felt like giving my uterus the middle finger, but little good it would do me now. After changing, I grabbed my purse from the table and darted back inside the bathroom. I always kept an emergency stash of supplies in my purse, but that wouldn't be enough to get me through. I'd need to find a store later.

As I took a moment to compose myself, the reality of the situation suddenly hit me. I was thirty years old, soon to be thirty-one, having irregular, spotty periods. My doctor had once mentioned that a women's fertility past age thirty wasn't something to trifle with.

I couldn't help noticing that my hands shook as I washed them. Something I'd never given much thought to—the desire to have a baby, to give a baby to this perfect man who I was falling in love with—suddenly felt very important. Mason wanted kids one day. What if I couldn't…? Would he still want me? I would never want to make him feel like he had to be with me if I couldn't be a mother.

I had to make the best of our remaining days, and then I needed to get myself to the doctor and pray everything would be okay.

Forcing a deep breath into my lungs, I tied on my swimsuit and fastened my hair into a ponytail.

"Mace?" I called, stepping out into the hallway. "Change of plans."

Chapter Twenty-Two

Mason

The convenience store was about the same size as a supply closet, though it offered even less selection than one. I walked inside and looked at the overpriced toiletries, then hastily grabbed what I needed and made my way to the counter in short order.

Behind the register, a young guy fiddled with his phone and he looked up as I approached.

"What's up, bro?" he said with a smile.

"Just needed to grab something," I told him, then set the box of tampons on the counter.

"Lady troubles, huh?" he asked, scanning the bright pink box.

I gritted a tight smile and the fool laughed.

"You must really love her if you're coming out here to buy her these," the kid joked. I just stared at him, waiting for him to hand me my bag. When he did, I forked over my cash, then headed back outside, suddenly all too aware of the guy's voice still playing in my head.

"You must really love her."

I, of course, was doing what any grown man should do in my situation, but the words still seemed to ring true. It wasn't a pipe dream or bullshit based on my parents' relationship. Not anymore.

I loved Bren.

I really did.

I loved the way she smiled and the way she laughed. I loved the way her face went blank when she was surprised. I even liked how she made me work to get beneath her hard outer-shell. The way she made a person feel like, if she was telling you something, it was because she'd decided you were one of the few people worthy of her trust. She was sensual and her body responded to my touch like no other. She was gorgeous, too. But then even that didn't matter to me much.

Without the baby, without the rest of the world, still all I wanted was her.

I rushed to the villa, determined not to scare her away with my big announcement but just as determined to show her how I felt. When I got there, I found her lounging on the beach in nothing but her bikini. The smooth, flat plane of her white stomach practically shone in the sun, and I dropped off the bag on the patio before making my way toward her.

"Got your supplies," I gestured toward the convenience store bag as I approached.

Bren chuckled. "I'm covered for now. But thank you."

"You're ridiculously beautiful, do you know that?" I asked, and she smiled up at me, her sunglasses covering the light in her eyes.

"What's got you in such a good mood?" she asked, and I sank to my knees beside her.

"You." I tucked a piece of her golden hair behind her ear. "Always you."

Her smile softened and I leaned over to kiss her, hoping to show her all the feelings that had overwhelmed me on the way here. In every push and pull of our mouths, I wanted her to know that I needed her, that she was everything to me.

"I want you," she murmured.

"Are you sure?" I asked.

She nodded.

"So have me."

Her tongue swept out to coax mine, and I savored every stroke. Weaving my fingers in the silky strands of her hair, I moved to cup the back of her neck, losing myself in the feel of her lips as she kissed me.

Slowly I worked the buttons of my shirt until I shrugged it off and let it fall onto the sand. We were utterly alone in front of the villa—miles from any other people—and I intended to make the most of it. I palmed the weight of her gorgeous breasts in my hands, but before I had the chance to pull away her bikini, she shook her head.

"I haven't forgotten last time. You wouldn't let me. But now…" She reached for my fly and unzipped it, then tugged my pants and boxers down in one motion.

"What do you mean?" I asked, and she guided me back down against the chaise lounge chair, kissing the hard muscles of my chest as she sank to her knees beside me.

"I want to taste you," she said. "You wouldn't let me the last time, but today I'm not taking no for an answer. It's been about me from the start. For once, let's make things about you."

I held my breath, trying to find the words to argue. I didn't care if she was on her period—at this point I wouldn't have cared if she had two heads. Before I found the words, though, her ass was in the air behind her and she was hovering over my thick, straining shaft.

Taking my length in one hand, she worked me slowly, gently, until finally her mouth closed over me and I let out a little groan of satisfaction.

"Bren." I tried to stop her, but then she bobbed deeper, taking as much of me in her mouth as she could while working the rest with her hand.

I let out a murmured curse as she gagged a little, and then I forced myself to thread my fingers through her hair again, willing myself to pull her away and focus instead on her pleasure. When I tried, though, she only released me with a little *pop* and shook her head.

"Not this time," she said. "I want to make you come."

"But—" I tried to argue, but she silenced me again by swirling the tip of her tongue around my swollen head, all the while staring deep into my eyes. Then, slowly licking her lips, she shook her head again.

"Don't you want to give me what I want?" she pouted.

"I—" I broke off, growling as she bobbed against my length, sucking hard and deep until my eyes dropped closed and I leaned back into the chair, trying to force myself to think of something, anything other than how good it would feel to spurt my hot need inside her mouth…feel her throat close over me.
I imagined how hot it would be to see my seed dripping down onto her breasts while she took me deeper inside her warm, wet mouth.

As I moved my hips in encouraging thrusts, her tongue stroked the underside of my shaft, stopping every now and then to tease the sensitive tip. In that moment, I would have given anything for her to rip off that bikini and let me watch her breasts bounce as she worked me up and down.

"You have no idea how hot you are," I groaned.

She smiled at me, though her hand never stopped its work. "Why don't you tell me?"

"You're the sexiest woman alive. Every time I lay eyes on you I want to tear your clothes off and have my way with you right then and there."

"Oh, yeah?" she cooed, rolling her tongue over my sensitive tip as I jerked into her mouth.

"Yes," I groaned. "Right now all I want is for you to take that top off and let me see your perfect breasts, baby."

"Do you know what I want?" she asked, and I struggled to breathe as I stared at the way she was working me over

"What's that?"

"I want you to come in my mouth and watch you lose control. How does that sound?"

I swallowed hard. "My girl gets what she wants."

The Soul Mate

"Good." She offered me a mischievous grin then sank to her knees again, taking as much of me in her mouth as she could and working me long and deep. This time there was no gentleness in her touch. No, she was all urgency and need and want, working me fast and hard and coaxing me toward the finish line.

Her tongue flicked over me, teasing me even as my balls drew up and I readied myself for her.

Staring into her eyes, I managed to grit out the words, "Going to come."

And she smiled around me, her tongue twisting over my tip as I jerked and threaded my hands through her hair. Closing my eyes, I focused on her warm, wet lips and groaned as the wave of pleasure shot through my body, rolling over me like the ocean waves in front of us.

In that moment, I lost control, flexing and pulsing as hot come spurted from my cock into her waiting throat. She never slowed, working me through it, taking me deeper as I came. I couldn't stop the deep guttural sound coming from my mouth that I didn't even recognize as my own. My vision blurred as I tried to find my breath again.

When I'd finally stopped twitching, she pulled away and lay beside me as I fought to catch my breath.

I turned toward her, relishing the swollen redness of her lips.

"Let's get married." The words slipped from my mouth before I'd thought them through, but there was no doubting I meant them. I wanted to spend every day of the rest of my life waking up next to her face. I wanted to have that baby we'd been so afraid of at first. I wanted everything—with her. But I knew it was risky. She was already gun-shy. What if this was the thing that sent her packing?

"What?" She laughed, sweeping her hair to one side before lying back on my chest.

"You heard me. I want you, Bren. Marry me."

This time, she sat up and met my eyes. "If that's the way you react to a blow job, you must not have had very many in your life," she joked, but her hand fluttered to her throat and her eyes gleamed.

A good sign?

"It wasn't that, although, shit, that was so damned good. It was you. Bren, I love you," I murmured. "Be my wife, baby."

She blinked at me, her eyes wide. "You haven't had time to think this through."

"I don't need time. I know that I love you. I've loved you since the first moment I saw you. I know this is fast, but we're perfect together."

She searched my gaze for a long moment, then shook her head and said, "Look, um, I think we're both a little high off the vacation fumes. I'm not saying no. I've never felt this way, to be honest. But I just want to make sure we're not rushing things. Let's put a pin in it, okay? Talk when we get home…"

I bit down on the inside of my cheek, looking her over as I nodded. Even now, I could feel her edging away from me, and the deep closeness I'd felt between us was crumbling like a wall made of sand.

Sure, marriage was fast and I knew she had her issues with intimacy, but I also knew how she felt about me—I could feel it in the way she kissed me, the way she touched me.

So why pull away?

"Bren," I said, but she was getting up and dusting herself off.

"I'm going to hit the shower and take a nap, okay?" she said.

I nodded. "You sure, baby? You okay?"

She nodded. "I'll see you in a little while."

I watched her march into the little outdoor shower, all the while wondering to myself if I ought to call her back and set the record straight. But there was nothing to fix. I loved her, but she hadn't said she loved me. And she hadn't agreed to marry me.

A knot formed deep in the pit of my stomach, the kind you get when you've done something rash while overwhelmed with emotion. I grabbed my shorts from the sand, pulling them on quickly before wading out into the low tide.

I'd jumped the gun because it felt right. I'd *wanted* to. I'd rushed it when I'd known how skittish she was, and now it remained to be seen what would happen from here.

Waves crashed in the distance. I heard the spray of the shower, but I closed my eyes, focusing instead on whether or not I'd just made the biggest mistake of my life.

Chapter Twenty-Three

Bren

I sat in the doctor's office, swinging my legs back and forth as I listened to the ticking of the clock on the wall behind me. In truth, the clock—along with my healthy sense of panic—was the only thing keeping me awake. I was still jet-lagged from the plane ride home yesterday, and though I'd briefly considered canceling the appointment, I knew it had nothing to do with my exhaustion.

No, it had to do with fear. A dark shadow of terror had taken root deep within me, coloring every one of my thoughts, and ever since we'd touched back down in the city, it had grown in strength, threatening to choke me from the inside out. At my age, the window for having children was already getting smaller. I knew that.

But to be having irregular periods at thirty?

It couldn't be a good sign.

Right?

I glanced again at the steel door handle, willing it to turn and allow the doctor inside. The nurse had already taken my temperature and weight along with my blood pressure and the other tests they did whenever I went into the office. With some luck, she wouldn't mention to anyone else who exactly the patient in exam room B was, but if she did...

Well, I'd worry about that later.

For now, I just had to put all my energy into willing that door open.

All this stress and worry could be for nothing, after all. I simply couldn't know for sure until the doctor appeared.

Which, after a few more menacing ticks of the clock, she did.

After glancing down at the tablet in her hand, she grinned at me and clicked the door closed. Carefully she made her way to the rolling stool in front of the little granite countertop in the room and then spun around to face me.

Slapping her hands against her knees, she said, "Well, Miss Matthews, I've taken a look at your chart and

I understand you're having a few concerns about your fertility, is that right?"

I gave her a shaky nod. "It's just that I got my period really late last month and then it only lasted a little while before disappearing again."

She pursed her lips, looking like she was concentrating deeply on every word I said, then tilted her head to the side, letting her brown ponytail spill onto the counter behind her.

"Has this over happened before?"

I nodded. "Once or twice."

"May I be frank with you, Miss Matthews?"

"Bren," I corrected her. "And yes, absolutely."

My stomach tightened and I linked my fingers together in my lap.

"You are right to be concerned about your fertility. At age thirty, sporadic or irregular periods tend not to be a good sign. But there's no reason to be scared, okay?"

No reason to be scared? I felt like she was the big bad wolf, blowing down my entire house of twigs and leaving nothing but a desolate patch of dirt in her wake. A whole plot of nothingness where not even a weed would grow. Mason's face, crumpled and disappointed, flashed through my mind, but I forced myself to nod and listen to what she had to say next.

"Now, it says on your chart that you're not looking to conceive anytime soon, but we can still run some tests and see what's going on. From there, we'll know what our options are."

"And if I'm—" I started, then choked on the words and tried again. "If I can't have a baby naturally, what are the options?"

The doctor hugged her tablet to her chest, crossing her arms over the top of it. "Well, if there's an issue, which there may not be, you might opt for an egg retrieval."

"What would that do?"

"Essentially, we would freeze your eggs for surrogacy or in vitro fertilization, depending on the particular issue with conception." The doctor nodded knowingly. "Also, now that you are thirty, it might be time to take conceiving a little more seriously. By thirty-six, your eggs could become geriatric, which would mean the option of freezing them would be off the table and, of course, any pregnancy you might have would be higher risk. It is six years away, but it's something to think about if you're serious about having children."

I nodded, trying to mask the heart-stopping panic oozing through my body like a disease. Taking a deep breath, I tried to speak, but the doctor held up a palm to stay me.

"Look, Bren. I know this is a lot. Just remember that it could have just been a one-off. Sometimes stress or diet or even environment can have a lot to do with our cycles. I wouldn't get too concerned about any of it just yet."

"You're sure?" I asked.

"Positive. Now, just to be on the safe side, I'm going to send in a nurse to get some samples for a fertility test, and I'll call you within a week or so to let you know the results. Good news or bad, you'll be hearing from me, so don't worry when you see me on your call list."

"Thank you, Doctor." My sigh of relief stuck in my throat and I leaned back again, staring at the ceiling as she slipped from the room and a nurse re-entered.

Closing my eyes, I waited as she explained the test to me. They already had a urine and blood sample, so the only thing they didn't have from me at this point was a piece of my soul. Then again, depending on the news the doctor gave me next week, they might take a bit of that as well.

When the nurse left, I got dressed quickly, then slipped from the room and ensured my copay was handled before sliding out of the practice and into the wide, silent atrium.

This, I knew, would be the most daunting part of my trip—even more so than the doctor's visit. Because, idiot that I was, I'd failed to notice that the doctor I'd scheduled my appointment with housed their offices just down the hall from Bentley Women's Medicine.

Of course, Mason would have already been in the office for hours by now, but that didn't make it any less nerve-wracking to walk past his etched glass double doors.

And when the bell on the door chimed behind me after I'd walked by, my heart leapt into my throat.

I debated whether to turn around and see my fate, but the decision was snatched from me when I heard a familiar, deep rumble of a voice behind me.

"Bren, what are you doing here?" Mason asked and I turned around, heat already surging to my cheeks.

"Nothing." I shook my head. "Nothing. I'm just heading out, actually. I didn't mean to interrupt your day."

"I was just about to go for lunch, actually. You want to join me?"

"Miss Matthews!" An airy female voice cut between us and I turned to find the nurse striding toward me with my jacket in her hand. "You left your coat," she said, then gave a polite nod to Mason.

"Dr. Bentley," she said.

"Hey, Marlene," he said back, and then she turned on her heel and strode back to her office.

Mason watched her for a long moment, then turned to face me, his gaze searching mine.

"What was that?" he asked.

The Soul Mate

"I had a doctor's appointment, that's all."

"And you didn't tell me?" he asked. It didn't take a genius to hear the hurt in his voice, like I'd betrayed him with some sort of sordid doctor switching affair, but I ignored it, squaring my shoulders as I took a deep breath.

"Look, I don't want to talk about this."

"There's not much of anything you do want to talk about," he shot back.

"What's that supposed to mean?"

"It means if something is wrong, I have the right to know. When two people care about each other and are trying to form a relationship, they share things."

I shook my head. "All I do is disappoint you, Mason. There isn't a baby tying us together anymore. Maybe it's better if we just take a break." I hoped he couldn't hear the pain in my voice. All I wanted to do was run. Because I could already feel my heart starting to crack. And when it shattered, I might not ever make my way back from the agony. Better to glue it back together myself, make a clean break and pray it stayed knit together.

"You don't mean that. After the island and—"

"What are you going to do? Charter a trip every time we're reminded of our real life circumstances? We'd never leave the place," I said. "I'm sorry, but I've got to go."

He tried to grab for my arm, but I pulled away and strode toward the revolving doors, not bothering to turn when he called after me. I'd made myself clear and—most important of all—I knew if I turned and saw his face, I would never be able to leave again.

But leaving was the right thing to do. Mason wanted children. I'd known it since the first moment I'd told him I might be pregnant, and even more so when we'd both been so let down when I wasn't.

And if I couldn't have them? Then what kind of monster would I be for leading him on and denying him the one thing he wanted most of all?

Biting back another swell of panic, I got in my car and drove to the one place I knew I'd be able to think through my options. The zoo was closed today as part of some conservationist holiday, but I knew that I'd be able to get in regardless.

When I got there, the parking lot was empty save for one bright orange Fiat. Mandy's car.

Jangling my keys as I walked, I let myself in and headed to my friend's office. It was empty.

Odd.

When she saw my car, there was no doubt she'd call, but for now I wanted to be alone anyway. Holding my breath, I made my way to the cheetah enclosure and stepped inside Cocoa and Nibs's shelter. Except rather than a great lumbering dog and its friendly cheetah companion, I found Mandy with a cheetah on her lap as she stroked him.

"What's going on?" I asked.

The cheetah didn't bother looking up at me, but Mandy pursed her lips, never stopping her soft strokes on the animal's head.

"Nibs died this morning," she murmured, her throat clogged with unshed tears.

I blinked, the breath leaving me in a whoosh. "What? No, he was in perfect health."

Mandy shook her head. "It was sudden. Looks like he had leukemia and we didn't see it."

My heart froze. "Poor Cocoa."

Mandy nodded. "We're going to try and bring in a new dog, but…"

She didn't have to say the rest. We all knew what usually became of the cheetahs who lived without their dogs and the dogs who lived without their cheetahs. The depression could set in, making it harder for them to eat or function. And eventually? It was that depression that could kill them.

I'd never felt more connected to one of the animals in the zoo in all my life. I had barely dodged this bullet with Mason myself and now, seeing this animal in so much pain, it was a much needed reminder that love fucking hurt.

Who needed that in their life?

Carefully I took a step toward Cocoa, and when she didn't move, I began to stroke her in time with Mandy.

"What brings you here on a holiday?" she asked. "I haven't told anyone about Nibs yet."

"No, I just came to visit them. I had a couple of things I wanted to think over and I thought this might be a nice place to do it."

Mandy nodded. "So the doctor's visit didn't go well?"

I sighed. "Not exactly."

"But they can't tell you anything until they run the tests. So now you wait and wonder, right?"

I nodded. "How'd you know?"

She offered me a small, sad smile. "Because I've been there."

"You…?" I asked and she nodded.

"A year after I got married, we decided we wanted to start a family, but…" She shrugged. "Well, things didn't happen like we thought they would. It took us seven years and several miscarriages to conceive. It was awful at the time, obviously. I felt like I'd let my husband down."

"I'm so sorry, Mandy. I can't believe you never told me," I said.

She shrugged. "It was a hard string of years, but it all worked out for us in the end."

I took a deep breath, held it, then let it out slowly. "Mason just wants a baby so damn bad."

"Is that what he said when you told him?"

"No." I didn't meet her eyes, because deep down, I knew I was just using my questionable fertility to wall myself off from something that terrified me. Love. A future. "I didn't tell him. I didn't want to see his expression. Don't want his pity."

"What about the sympathy?" Mandy asked.

"Is there a difference?"

"Only one way to find out," Mandy said, then led Cocoa onto my lap and dusted herself off. "Look, I've got to get going. Make sure you lock up when you leave, all right?"

I nodded, watching her go, but then she turned around again and said, "You can't live your life in fear, kid."

"What if it's the only thing distracting me from how my heart is breaking?" I asked, and her eyes turned soft.

"Sometimes, you have to let it break. That's the only way it's going to heal. Like a hangnail. Rip it off and let the skin grow back."

I laughed, a hollow sound. "That's a terrible metaphor."

"They don't pay me to be a wordsmith." She backed out of the enclosure, and I stared down at the cheetah in my lap for another long moment, stroking her fur as she mewled sadly.

First I'd lost my father. Now I might have lost the chance to become a mother myself—the chance to ever have a family of my own that would be full and happy and complete.

The impulse to languish and dissolve into my predicament, just like my mother had done, was strong, almost overwhelming. But then, my mother had allowed herself to dive into her grief, and what had it done for her? Even now, years later, she was letting life drift past her, unlived.

Grieving was a process, not a life sentence and, no matter what the doctor said, I was going to have to face the facts of my father's death and my own ability to be a mother.

But I didn't have to do it alone.

Not for the first time, I thought of Mason that day in the sand, my hand in his as he asked me to be his wife. He'd booked a trip just for me. He'd gone out of his way over and over again for my sake.

And what had I done for him? Nothing. I hadn't even done him the courtesy of letting him know how I felt.

That was something I could change, though.

And for the first time in my life? I wanted to talk about it.

Chapter Twenty-Four
Mason

This was it. The end of the line.

After everything we'd been through—all the ways I'd thought fate had led her to me—Bren had walked away like I'd been nothing to her. Slowly, like the weight of the world was on my shoulders, I walked back into my office and asked my assistant to hold my calls until further notice.

Then, when I was sure I was completely and totally alone, I slid open the top drawer of my desk and pulled out the ring box I'd gotten just this morning. Inside, the diamond solitaire sparkled up at me and I studied the intricate silver filigree of the band, all while trying my hardest not to toss the damn thing across the room. My stomach cramped and I let out a snarl.

How could I have been so stupid?

She'd given me every indication she wasn't ready, throwing up flags in every shade of red on the color wheel. And I'd chosen to ignore them all. Gritting my teeth, I shoved the ring back in my desk and stalked toward the door. I couldn't see patients today, not like this, and there was only one place I knew I could go to calm down.

"Cancel my appointments. I'm not feeling well today," I said to my assistant, then headed out the door and toward my car without looking a single person in the eye.

Revving the engine, I pulled onto the interstate, following the familiar highway exits until I pulled up in front of the brick building I knew so well. The trees in front of the place swayed in the wind, and I glanced at them briefly. Then I made my way to the door and used the knocker.

First once, then again, I raised the heavy gold handle and let it drop, waiting to hear footfalls on the other side of the door. On the third try, I finally heard the light pitter-patter of someone's feet on the wood floor, so I took a step back and waited for my mother to open the door.

When she did, there was no way I could hold back a moment longer.

"I have to talk to you."

She led me inside, and before she'd even begun to pour the coffee I was admitting to the entire sordid tale. The way I'd looked for Bren after our one-night stand, the imagined pregnancy, the trip I'd planned. Even things most men might not admit to their mothers, I told her, if only so that she might unearth some small detail I'd overlooked so I could make things right.

"Wow, this girl really seems like something," my mother said when I was finally finished.

"She's not just something—she's everything."

Mom smiled sadly. "That was a lot for one person to take in in one sitting. I didn't know I was almost a grandma, after all."

I nodded. "I just don't understand why she'd make an appointment with Marlene Thomas instead of me and then not tell me about it."

My mother raised her eyebrows. "*That's* the part you can't figure out?"

"Well, yeah." I shrugged. "Is there something else?"

"Are you serious?" She took a long sip of her coffee, surveying me over the top of her mug. "Sometimes you really are your father's son, you know that?"

"I'm guessing that's not a compliment given the impending divorce, huh?"

My mother smiled. "Your father is kind and smart and funny in all the best ways. But when it comes to women…well, frankly, when he told me what he did for a living, I couldn't believe it."

"What's that supposed to mean?"

"Well, first of all, mister, isn't it obvious why she didn't come to you or tell you?" She pursed her lips, then began ticking off items on her fingers. "A thirty-year-old woman with irregular periods. What do you think she went to the doctor for?"

I blinked. "I don't…"

"Then they shouldn't have let you graduate from medical school," she said with a warm smile that took the edge off. "I've been married to a doctor long enough to tell you what that girl was doing and I don't even have a degree."

"You think it was a fertility thing?" I asked, flipping through the conversation with Bren in my mind as a cold ball of dread formed in my stomach. For the first time since I'd ran into her at my office, logic trumped emotion.

"Well, if you had a patient with her background, what kind of tests would you run?"

The truth of her words sank into my skin and I sat back, thinking hard. "But, okay, even if she went for a fertility test, why wouldn't she have come to me?"

"The man whose baby she thought she was carrying not a week before? Hardly the natural choice, don't you think? You told her you were disappointed about not having a baby. Do you think she wanted to make you the person who told her she might never have a baby?"

My breath caught in my chest and, slowly, I shook my head. "I guess I never thought of it that way."

"That's the way it is." My mother set her coffee down on the table between us, then rested back against the sofa cushions. "So, sweetheart, it makes complete sense why she went to Dr. Thomas."

"But that's not the part I should be wondering about?"

She shook her head.

"Care to enlighten me, oh wise one?" I asked.

She folded her hands together. After letting out one long breath, she said, "Haven't you wondered what's going on in this girl's head that every time you get close to her, she freaks out and runs away?"

"Well, she told me she got weird about intimacy."

"Yes, but why? What do you know about her past? Any boyfriends who left her? If her parents' relationship was bad?"

"Shit." Icy realization crept down my spine. The most important relationship a woman had was with her father. Bren had lost hers at a young age, before she'd matured into a successful adult and long before she was ready. I couldn't even imagine what it felt like to lose a parent, especially during those angsty teenage years.

Mom continued on. "I imagine you told her about my cancer and the divorce, but she never reciprocated at all?"

I blinked, trying to focus in on my mother's words in a way that might force them to make sense. "She lost her father," I finally uttered.

Mom nodded. "She has a fear of abandonment. My suggestion is to go to her. The longer you let her stew in her thoughts, the more she's going to convince herself she did the right thing by leaving you. Whatever is making her run isn't going away anytime soon. In order to open her warm, loving center, you're going to need to peel away her fear layer by layer. If she's worth it, you have to try."

I nodded. "I will. Thanks, Mom."

She rose from the couch, giving my shoulder a soft pat. "Anytime. You actually caught me on my way out."

I hugged my mother goodbye and set off for my place, the desperate need to see Bren almost making me pull a U-turn and go straight to her place. But I needed a moment to think, to come up with a plan—figure out the right words to say. I wasn't about to let us end like this. I'd spent my whole life searching for my one perfect mate, and I'd finally found her. I just had to make her see it.

When I pulled to a stop in front of my place, Bren's car was already parked outside. The sky outside was turning an ominous shade of gray and a rumble of thunder vibrated in the distance.

"Bren," I breathed. "I didn't expect to find you here."

She shoved a strand of golden hair behind her ear. "Sorry, I had a lot on my mind and when I got in my car, I just drove. I ended up here." She let out a massive sigh, her eyes just as dark and stormy as the sky overhead.

"It's fine. I was thinking we should talk too."

A crack of thunder made Bren flinch.

"Come on." I tugged her toward the house.

Once inside we toed off our shoes and I lead her into the living room. "Something to drink?" I asked as we passed the kitchen. Bren shook her head, stopping in front of the windows.

For a moment we just stared at each other, neither one wanting to break the charged silence.

"You were right," we said the words in unison, then met eyes, both of us afraid to laugh.

I hesitated, waiting for Bren to speak, and then she offered me a small smile and began.

"There are certain things about me that I don't like to share with people. But now… with you . . . " She shook her head.

I smiled but didn't speak. I wanted her to be open to telling me whatever she had on her mind.

"I told you about my dad on the plane, but I guess I left out the parts about how it affected me."

My stomach dropped, but I stayed quiet as she rushed to continue.

"He was diagnosed when I was twelve, and for three years I watched my mother at his bedside day and night."

She paused, but I still said nothing, waiting for her to give me some signal that it was all right for me to talk. For now, this was her time and it was long overdue, so I nodded encouragingly, despite the urge to drag her into my arms and comfort her.

"So, for those three years, it was like I was losing both of my parents at once, you know? My mother's attention was elsewhere, my father was slowly losing the ability to do the things we used to do together like go fishing or fix cars. Then, when he died…" Her voice broke, and I waited as she cleared her throat and started again.

"When he died, it was like both my parents had gone. Even now, so many years later, my mom can barely function without him. And while I was in the cheetah enclosure, I was thinking about that sort of loss, you know? When cheetahs' companions die, they languish and die, too. And ever since my father died, I've been afraid that that is sort of the fate of people who fall in love. You get left behind eventually and it's not like I can ask you not to die, you know?"

A slow tear trickled down her cheek and I took a step forward, then grasped her hand and squeezed it.

She let me hold her hand, and continued. "I know it must have seemed crazy to you with things going so well and me just slipping away all the time. It's just that I can feel myself falling for you and I can't bear to lose you, you know? And as we get closer, it's only going to get worse and when you leave…" Another tear slid down her cheek and she wiped it away hastily.

"I just don't want to lose myself the way she—my mom—did."

"You didn't do that when your father died," I offered.

She met my gaze wearily. "I did, though. I was a mess for an entire year."

"But now?" I shook my head. "You're not. You can't live your life running from grief just like I can't promise to never die. But if you avoid things that make you happy for fear of losing them, then you'll never be truly happy to begin with."

"I know." She nodded. "It's just really hard for me. To be near you and know that anything could happen. And when we didn't have the baby, I just thought, well, I thought I'd lost something all over again. Even though I never had anything to lose. It felt like—"

"I know exactly what you mean," I said. "But there will be other chances."

"Maybe not," she said, and the silent tears became a gasping sob.

"Bren…"

"I'm thirty," she choked, refusing to be consoled. "And with the unpredictable cycles—"

I hushed her, then looped my arm around her shoulder and guided her toward the couch. When we were settled, she rested her head on my shoulder and I stroked her hair, silent and waiting for her to find her voice again.

"What if I can't have children?" she whispered.

"You won't know until the tests come in, but even if you can't? There are options. Lots and lots of options. This isn't the end."

"But I'd be letting you down," she choked, and I tucked my hand under her chin, lifting her eyes to meet mine.

"The only way you'd ever let me down is if you run away from everything we could share without even trying to explore how beautiful it could be. I don't need to have a baby. I don't need to have anything except for you. You know that?"

She shook her head. "I didn't."

"I want you in my life. I want to spend every day with you, and what I said when I proposed? I meant it.

You're the best, most incredible thing that's ever happened to me."

"Then ask me again."

"What?"

"Ask me again." She sniffled.

I laughed. "I don't have your ring with me." It was in my bedroom, tucked away in a box at the top of my closet.

"I don't care. Just ask me."

So I did. Bending onto one knee in the middle of the room, I took her left hand, stroking her naked ring finger. "Bren, I love every inch of you and I never want to leave your side for as long as I live. Become my wife, baby?"

She nodded, still sniffling, then took my hand. "Yes, of course. I want nothing more than to marry you."

Grinning like an idiot, I swept my hand through Bren's hair, pulling her toward me for a soft, heart-stopping kiss. Then, trailing kisses along her jaw, I paused near the shell of her ear and whispered, "From here on out, in sickness and in health, we live every day in the present. What may come, may come."

She nodded. "What may come, may come."

"Now come here. It's been too long." Taking her hand in mine, I dragged her down the hall, all too eager to make up for every lost moment we'd spent apart.

I led her to my bedroom and paused in the center of the room, turning her to face the large mirror that hung on the wall beside my dresser. Taking my time, I stripped Bren of every article of clothing she wore—today it was a knee-length skirt and cream silk blouse. I loved how sweet and feminine she was, yet tough at the same time. Once her clothes were on the floor at her feet, I dropped to my knees, worshipping her with soft kisses and teasing licks to all the spots that made her knees tremble.

"Mason," she groaned, pushing a hand into my hair.

When I finally led her to bed, it was with the striking clarity that this was exactly where she belonged. I'd spent all those miserable weeks searching for her—and that was after just one night together. I didn't want to tell her, but losing her scared me just as badly. Maybe even more. Because I'd already envisioned it all—our beautiful life, her by my side, maybe babies someday.

We made love with fiery passion the first time, my cock was eager to show my new fiancé how much he missed her. The second time was slower, tender, and perfect. And when we were done I made her stay put while I jogged naked to the closet, Bren laughing at my bare behind and shouting at me to come back to bed.

But when I returned moments later with her ring, Bren's protests died on her lips, and with tears gathering in her eyes, I slid it onto her finger where it belonged.

Chapter Twenty-Five

Bren

"Shoes or no shoes?" I stared down at the glittery gold sandals that had seemed perfect at the department store, but now felt like overkill.

"Whatever you'll be most comfortable in," Mandy said. "It is the beach after all."

"Barefoot it is." I kicked the sandals to the side and grabbed my bouquet from the dresser.

The white lace dress was fitted all the way down to my thighs, where it then jutted out just slightly. I'd known it was the one from the first moment I saw it in the store. Mandy's bridesmaid dress was seafoam green and looked beautiful on her.

"Are you ready?" she asked.

I nodded, suddenly more eager than excited. "Let's do this."

"You good if I go out for a minute and check if everything is ready?" Mandy asked.

I nodded, glancing in the mirror one last time. "I'm good."

And I was. My heart was full and happy, and I felt incredibly blessed.

Mandy stepped out and I applied one last coat of lipstick, inspecting my reflection while trying to wait patiently, and failing miserably.

"Bren?" Mason's deep voice called. He stepped through the door, looking delicious and handsome in his camel-colored linen suit and pale blue shirt. My heart throbbed with love for the man about to become my husband. If I allowed my mind to drift back to how we almost didn't make it here…I shook my head. Not today. Today was going to be the best day of my life. No uncomfortable memories and no regrets. Well, maybe just one regret. My incredible dad wouldn't be here to walk me down the aisle toward my future.

"What are you doing here? It's bad luck to see the bride before the wedding."

He shook his head, a smile tugging up his lips. "You look so beautiful, Bren. And I told you, there's no such thing as bad luck with us. Soul mates, right?"

He crossed the room toward me and drew me into his arms.

A happy smile overtook my mouth. He'd told me that when he proposed the second time. It was an overly romantic affair, one that had me crying and sobbing yes, over and over. Especially when he slid the stunning ring onto my finger.

"Well, what are you doing in here, darling soul mate? Did you need something?"

His eyes darkened. "Just wanted to see you before all the commotion started. Everyone says their wedding day goes by too fast. I don't want to look back on this day and have it be a blur. I want to remember every second I can get with you."

My heart jumped in my chest at his sweet words, and those stolen moments together took on new meaning. He didn't have something important to tell me. He just wanted to see me.

"I can't wait 'til everyone's gone." He chuckled, pulling me in close.

"That's awful! They all just got here." We'd rented the same house we had last time we were here on Grand Cayman, only this time we also rented the house next door.

"I know, and I'm already looking forward to them leaving in a few days so I can have you all to myself."

I pressed a small kiss to his mouth. "I love you."

"Love you more," he murmured. It was his

standard answer ever since we became so open with our declarations. And even though it still felt a little strange for me to be so forthcoming, it also felt...good. Right.

Mason had opened me up, and under his unending love and gentle pressure, I'd blossomed. I was no longer afraid to love, no longer afraid to live. We got only one shot at life, and I wasn't going to waste it anymore. Our close call with the pregnancy really opened up my eyes to a lot of things.

"I can't wait until we move in together," he added.

I'd dug my heels in and kept my own apartment, opting to keep living apart until we were married. We'd bought a house together last month and Mason had been living there alone, fixing it up. But I wanted something else to look forward to after the wedding. The truth was, I couldn't wait to move in.

"We have a lifetime together," I told him, stroking the stubble on his jaw. "Now shoo. Go. We have a wedding to attend." I gave his chest a pat and led him to the door.

"See you out there, Mrs. Bentley."

My mouth curled into a grin. "See you soon, Dr. Bentley."

Epilogue
Mason

All afternoon, I'd spent my time either putting the final touches on the nursery or convincing Bren not to jump on a pogo stick to see if it would force the babies out. For weeks now she'd been taking walks around the neighborhood, trying to kick-start her labor, but so far it had done nothing but make her cranky and exhausted.

Not that I could blame her. Being overdue for ten days was hard for anyone, but being overdue with twins? As far as I could tell, that was a fate worse than death.

Dutiful husband that I was, though, I'd made sure the bags were packed and in the trunk, the doctor was on speed dial, and both nurseries were ready for the babies. Though we'd initially thought about a blue one and a pink one, Bren wanted something that spoke to both of us. So our son's room had a little fisherman's cottage and tepee for him to play in while our daughter had a safari-style room with a giraffe my mother had painted watching over her from her crib.

I adjusted our daughter's mobile—all different colored parrots—then started as I heard the front door slam.

"Contractions!" Bren shouted and I rushed into the living room, my eyes wide.

You'd have thought that after the number of babies I'd brought into the world, I would know how to keep calm at a time like this, but no. Things changed in the blink of an eye when my own family's safety was involved. My heart jumped into my throat and I clenched my fists at my sides to keep my hands from shaking.

"How far apart?" I demanded.

"Don't know. Had the first one a few minutes ago." Bren looked at me with wild eyes and I took her arm, guiding her back toward the couch.

"No, don't. What if my water breaks?"

"Then we'll get a new couch. I want you to be comfortable. Put your feet up and I'll get you some water."

"But if we go to the hospital now, won't they induce labor?" she cried.

"You know we can't go until they're five minutes apart."

"But what if we go when they're five minutes apart and I get fully dilated and the babies fall out in the car?"

"You'll be with someone who knows how to deliver them. Which, technically, I should be doing anyway."

She rolled her eyes. "Yeah right, Dr. Big Shot. I'm not letting you near my hoo-ha unless it's in prime condition."

"You don't think you're being a little—?"

"No, I don't," she said, then clutched her stomach and began to moan in pain.

I hurried to grab her a cup and the stopwatch I'd kept in the kitchen since the seventh month of pregnancy—it never hurt to be too prepared—then rushed to her side and gave her the water.

"Thanks," she breathed when she'd finished, and she leaned farther back against the overstuffed cushions before grabbing the cup and taking a long drink.

"There are some things I need you to do for me when we get there," Bren said matter-of-factly.

"What's that?"

"You know the nice nurse, Suzy?"

I nodded.

"She's the one who's going to be in the room with the doctor, okay? And make sure you're extra nice to her so she gets me the good drugs."

"I'm pretty sure Trent already has the good drugs set aside for you."

She wrinkled her nose.

"What?"

"I'm still not crazy about your best friend delivering our baby."

"He's the second-best doctor in the city. You already said no to the first."

"Because you are going to be right by my side so I can swear at you for getting me in this predicament."

"I wouldn't have it any other way." I beamed, but then Bren clutched her stomach again and closed her eyes as she breathed through another contraction.

I'd been in this situation many times—always detached and professional—but now, seeing the woman I loved in physical pain, an ache inside my chest bloomed and for the first time ever, I had to force myself to relax and not worry.

I clicked the stopwatch, trying to stay calm for Bren's sake. "Four minutes. You know what that means."

She let out a long breath, then smoothed her hand over her stomach. "Time to get these kids out of me?"

"Yep." I grinned. "Time to have our babies."

Years of planning and it had all come down to this, this, and it was go time. I wouldn't leave my wife's side, would see to it that she was well cared for and attended to.

As I helped her into the car, I stared back at our little suburban house with the white picket fence and found myself grinning. By tomorrow, we'd be a family of four, healthy and happy and safe. I'd gotten here the strangest way possible, but now that I was here?

There was no way on Earth I ever wanted to leave. It was like every childhood fantasy I'd ever harbored about my future had morphed into a vibrant, technicolor life. The only thing missing were the two tiny humans we were about to meet.

"Dammit, Mason, drive, would you!" Bren groaned, clutching her round belly again.

I stepped on the gas, flooring the pedal as we sped off for the hospital, driving carefully even though my racing heart demanded that I run every red light in the city. Taking one hand off the wheel, I reached over and squeezed her hand. "Relax, baby. Breathe for me. You've got this."

Bren inhaled slowly and deeply, closing her eyes in the seat next to me.

We arrived at the hospital and Trent's calming demeanor set us both at ease. Eight hours later, two six-pound babies were nestled into the same basinet—one swaddled in a pink blanket, the other in blue while I laid beside Bren in the hospital bed, holding her close

They were pink-skinned and healthy, each with a swath of downy-soft brown hair.

"I'm so insanely proud of you," I murmured, kissing her hair. "They're perfect. Just like you."

"Are you sure you're not scared for life? You did just watch me deliver twins—*vaginally*," she emphasized.

I let out a soft chuckle and pulled her even closer. "Not even a little. I always thought it was pretty amazing what I did for a living—seeing life brought into this world—but I never understood the gravity of it, never felt such immense pride before. Watching you today was incredible."

I looked down at Bren and wiped away a stray tear from her cheek. The look in her eyes was pure love.

"I couldn't have done it without you," she

murmured.

She had been so scared to let me in, so afraid to fall in love, and I knew today that she'd finally surrendered to it completely. Because she wasn't just in love with me, we had added two new family members, and I could feel how much she loved them already. Her motherly instincts kicking in from the first moments she nuzzled the babies on her bare chest—nurturing them with skin to skin contact and attempting to nurse them.

"And I couldn't have done this without you. You're my soulmate, Bren."

I caught another tear with my thumb.

"Damn hormones. I'm sorry I'm crying," she said with the perfect little sniffle. For a woman who'd struggled expressing her emotions, she'd come a long way.

"I've got you. These next few weeks are going to be rough, but I'm here, and I'll never let you go."

Placing my lips against Bren's forehead, I felt her exhale and relax. She'd made all of my dreams come true, and I couldn't wait to spend the rest of my life showing her just how grateful I was.

Deleted Bonus Scene

Mason

Magical unicorn pussy.

That was the only way to describe what I was feeling.

It was hard to put into words without sounding all sentimental, but this was the best sex of my life, with the hottest woman I'd ever had in my bed.

As tight as she was, I was drilling into her, burying myself up to the hilt time and again. I hadn't found many women who could take all of me, and no one as snug as Bren.

Pure heaven.

"You okay with taking it deep like that, sweetheart?"

"Yeah," she panted. "Right there. Don't you dare stop."

Never. "I wouldn't dream of it," I grunted.

Lifting her knee so I could get even closer, I flexed my hips, sinking even further into her hot, willing body.

"I'm going to come again," she moaned beneath me.

I felt like thumping my chest. "You normally pull hat tricks like this?" I grunted out through gritted teeth.

"No, I'm sorry."

She was sorry? I would have forced out a laugh if my own climax wasn't charging at me like an angry bull.

"Go for it, baby," I encouraged. I loved how she took what she needed. There was nothing shy or timid about her. I could get addicted to being inside her. Hell, I could get addicted to *her*. "I've got all night."

"But this is number four…I feel like a freak," she murmured, burying her face against my throat. "This has never happened to me."

"You're perfect," I told her, and not for the first time tonight.

Knowing I hit all the right spots inside her? Knowing she was multi-orgasmic—just for me? It was everything a man wanted to hear, but I knew she wasn't just stroking my ego. I'd felt the way she trembled in my arms, every pulse each time she came and clamped down around me like a vise.

Moments later, Bren cried out again, and this time her release triggered my own, sparks shooting through my veins as I came harder than I ever had in my entire life.

Heart pounding, I rolled to my back, pulling her on top of me. Bren rested her head on my bicep and patted my chest.

"That was …"

"Yeah," I grunted, tugging her closer. There were no words for what that was. We might have to invent a few of our own come morning—call Webster's—have them added to the dictionary.

She let out a soft, happy sigh, making herself comfortable.

My eyes fell closed, and I held her there, content and warm. As soon as I caught my breath, I wanted a repeat.

I was just going to rest my eyes for a second. When my heart rate calmed down and I got my breathing under control enough to speak, I was going to get down on one knee to propose marriage, because holy fuck. This woman was it for me. She'd ruined me for all others, and I was going to make her mine. There were no other options. As crazy as it sounded, a pack of wild horses couldn't drag me away. I would make this woman mine come hell or high water. I would put a ring on her finger, my babies in her belly, and we'd live happily ever after.

Just watch me.

The End

Dr. & Mrs. Bentley, along with their sweet twins,
Gwen and Jacob thank you for reading!

Kisses,
Kendall

Acknowledgments

I wanted to say a massive thank-you to the readers who have been part of the Roommates series from the beginning. You guys seriously rock! I had so much fun writing this romantic comedy series and watching each couple get their happily-ever-after, including all the laughs, awkward moments, and sexy kisses along the way.

My team is the best, and I owe the following people a tremendous amount of thanks. Sara Eirew, Danielle Sanchez, Alyssa Garcia, and also to Jennifer Echols and Tami Stark for their editing guidance.

Thank you also to super fan, avid reader, and zoologist Susanne Gigler for being an early beta reader and making sure I wasn't going too far outside the realm of possibility with Bren's career of choice.

Next I want to tell you a little about my next series! It's hotter, grittier, and filled with more delicious angst, and best of all, the books are longer! I'm all about writing romantic sagas right now. As a writer, I love to constantly change things up and challenge myself. It's how I stay engaged and keep things fresh after writing 25+

novels. For that reason, I'm changing gears from writing romantic comedies and diving into a seductive and mysterious world about three alpha male brothers who own an escort agency. I am absolutely in LOVE with this series. The title of the series is Forbidden Desires, and book one is Dirty Little Secret. I can't wait to share it with you. And for those of you who love romantic comedies, don't worry—because I've got several of those planned too. Okay, now back to the writing cave!

Up Next . . .
Dirty Little Secret

Forbidden Desires Book One

Gavin Kingsley burst into my life in a sharp and unexpected twist of fate. You know his type—arrogant, dangerously handsome, and impossible to ignore.

Something dark within him calls to the shadows inside me. I long for the kind of heart-wrenching passion I've only read about, and his tragic past reads like one of my favorite literary classics. Raw. Visceral. Captivating. Together, we're a perfect mess.

The deeper I fall into his world, the more I crave him like a drug—he pushes every boundary I have, and challenges everything I thought I wanted. I want to unlock his heart. I want his dirty secrets.

But in the end, will he be the blade that cuts me . . . or the bond that makes my life complete?

Written in the same vein as Kendall Ryan's New York Times bestselling and much-loved international phenomenon, Filthy

Beautiful Lies, Dirty Little Secret begins an erotic new series.

Learn more about this series, and get your copy:
www.forbiddendesiresseries.com

Other Books in This Series

THE ROOM MATE

The last time I saw my best friend's younger brother, he was a geek wearing braces. But when Cannon shows up to crash in my spare room, I get a swift reality check.

Now twenty-four, he's broad shouldered and masculine, and so sinfully sexy, I want to climb him like the jungle gyms we used to enjoy. At six-foot-something with lean muscles hiding under his T-shirt, a deep sexy voice, and full lips that pull into a smirk when he studies me, he's pure temptation.

Fresh out of a messy breakup, he doesn't want any entanglements. But I can resist, right?

I'm holding strong until the third night of our new arrangement when we get drunk and he confesses his biggest secret of all: he's cursed when it comes to sex. Apparently he's a god in bed, and women instantly fall in love with him.

I'm calling bullshit. In fact, I'm going to prove him wrong, and if I rack up a few much-needed orgasms in the process, all the better.

There's no way I'm going to fall in love with Cannon. But once we start ... I realize betting against him may have been the biggest mistake of my life.

The Playmate

Smith Hamilton has it all—he's smart, good-looking, and loaded. But he remembers a time when he had nothing and no one, so he's not about to mess up, especially with his best friend's little sister. That means keeping Evie at arm's length ... even though the once pesky little girl is now a buxom bombshell. A sexy blonde who pushes his self-control to the limit the night she crawls into bed with him.

Evie Reed knows she's blessed—with an exclusive education, a family who loves her, and a new job managing social media for her family's lingerie company. But she wants more, like a reason to wear the sexy lingerie herself. She has just the man in mind to help with that. She's crushed on Smith forever. Surely tricking her way into his bed will force him to see her in a new, adult way.

Except that when Evie's plan leads to disaster, she

and Smith must decide—ignore the attraction sizzling between them, or become play mates and risk it all.

HOUSE MATE

What's sexier than a bad boy? A badass man who's got his shit together.

Max Alexander is nearing thirty-five. He's built a successful company and conquered the business world, but he's never been lucky in love. Focusing so much time on his business and raising his daughter, adulting has come at the expense of his personal life.

His social skills are shit, his patience is shot, and at times, his temper runs hot.

The last thing he has time for is the recently single, too-gorgeous-for-her-own-good young woman he hires to take care of his little girl. She's a distraction he doesn't need, and besides, there's no way she'd be interested.

But you know what they say about assumptions?

About the Author

A *New York Times*, *Wall Street Journal*, and *USA TODAY* bestselling author of more than two dozen titles, Kendall Ryan has sold over two million books, and her books have been translated into several languages in countries around the world. Her books have also appeared on the *New York Times* and *USA TODAY* bestseller lists more than three dozen times. Ryan has been featured in publications such as *USA TODAY*, *Newsweek*, and *In Touch Magazine*. She lives in Texas with her husband and two sons.

Website: www.kendallryanbooks.com

Other Books by Kendall Ryan

Unravel Me
Make Me Yours
Working It
Craving Him
All or Nothing
When I Break Series
Filthy Beautiful Lies Series
The Gentleman Mentor
Sinfully Mine
Bait & Switch
Slow & Steady
The Room Mate
The Play Mate
The House Mate
The Bed Mate
The Soul Mate
Hard to Love
Reckless Love
Resisting Her
The Impact of You
Screwed
Monster Prick
The Fix Up

For a complete list of Kendall's books, visit:
www.kendallryanbooks.com/all-books

Printed in Great Britain
by Amazon